"I want y... going to ...

Marcy was terrified by the determined sound of Randal's voice. Instinctively she backed away from him, warned by the dangerous gleam in his eyes.

She felt an increasing helplessness in the face of his ardent pursuit. Totally inexperienced with men, she had not yet felt the fierce touch of passion. Randal's lovemaking had puzzled and alarmed her.

Had he been a boy of her own age, she might have been able to cope. She might have enjoyed being led gently into love. But Randal Saxton was a powerful and experienced man, and he was forcing her into a situation she wasn't ready for....

WELCOME
TO THE WONDERFUL WORLD
OF *Harlequin Romances*

Interesting, informative and entertaining,
each Harlequin Romance portrays an appealing
and original love story. With a varied array
of settings, we may lure you on an African safari,
to a quaint Welsh village or an exotic Riviera
location—anywhere and everywhere that adventurous
men and women fall in love.

As publishers of Harlequin Romances, we're
extremely proud of our books. Since 1949,
Harlequin Enterprises has built its publishing
reputation on the solid base of quality and
originality. Our stories are the most popular
paperback romances sold in North America; every
month, six new titles are released and sold at
nearly every book-selling store in Canada and the
United States.

A free catalogue listing all available Harlequin Romances
can be yours by writing to the

HARLEQUIN READER SERVICE,
(In the U.S.) M.P.O. Box 707, Niagara Falls, N.Y. 14302
(In Canada) Stratford, Ontario, Canada N5A 6W2

or use coupon at back of book.

We sincerely hope you enjoy reading
this Harlequin Romance.

Yours truly,

THE PUBLISHERS
  Harlequin Romances

Sweet Compulsion

by

VICTORIA WOOLF

Harlequin Books

TORONTO • LONDON • NEW YORK • AMSTERDAM
SYDNEY • HAMBURG • PARIS

Original hardcover edition published in 1979
by Mills & Boon Limited

ISBN 0-373-02273-5

Harlequin edition published July 1979

CHAPTER ONE

LIKE a Pied Piper leading a yelling band of grimy London urchins up and down outside the Town Hall; bright yellow jeans, dusty sneakers on her feet—from the Mayor's Parlour it was hard to decide if she was a girl or a boy, except that by now everyone in the borough knew perfectly well that her name was Marcy Campion, and she was the girl from Paradise Street.

'I feel like Adolf Hitler,' said the Mayor to his secretary.

Miss Pierce surveyed his small neat face and bald head as if watching for signs of an incipient moustache.

The handwritten banners dipped and swayed below. A little huddle of photographers and reporters converged upon the slight figure in yellow jeans. The Mayor groaned.

Behind him the telephone rang. Miss Pierce picked it up, spoke briefly, then handed it to him with an expressionless face.

'Mr Saxton.'

The Mayor gave a hunted look around the room. The heavy, polished furniture reflected what traces of sunshine remained after it had been filtered through the dust-laden London air. A massive Victorian clock ticked ponderously on the marble mantelshelf. A portrait of the monarch gazed from a corner.

Reluctantly the Mayor lifted the receiver to his ear. The ghost of an obsequious smile drifted over his face as he spoke into it.

Mr Saxton had just, it seemed, read his newspaper. It had spoilt his breakfast.

The Mayor winced. 'Most unfortunate, yes . . . but . . . of course, I see that . . . but . . . you don't understand . . . oh, certainly . . . yes . . . naturally we want to co-operate, but . . .'

Miss Pierce gazed from the window. Kids need space, not office blocks, shouted one banner. Say no to big business, cried another.

Would it rain before lunch? thought Miss Pierce, studying the sky. There were clouds gathering in the west. She had not brought an umbrella and her tan suit showed every mark.

In the oak-panelled boardroom of Saxton and Company the directors talked about Marcy Campion in tones of incredulous irritation. There were six of them around the long, highly polished mahogany table; pin-striped, crisp-shirted, affluent. Five of them talked all at once, competing explosively. The sixth leaned back in his chair at the head of the table, narrowed blue eyes fixed on the painting which hung on the opposite wall; a painting long familiar to him in every detail, yet always fascinating because, for all the artist's skill, it failed to reveal the character of the subject.

Against an aptly stormy background he posed, casually, on the tilting deck of an eighteenth-century merchantman, his plum-coloured velvet coat and lace jabot richly glowing against the flying spray and massive waves. One slender white hand gripped the ship's wheel. The other was placed upon his hip. The effect was of staggering insolence—the dark, bold countenance stared out in challenge at the world, defying curiosity. Pirate, genius, unhung villain—all manner of descriptions had been applied by his contemporaries to the founder of the firm of Saxton and Company. James Saxton had grown enormously wealthy by exporting and importing—how exactly was uncertain. If his own century had not pierced the fierce mask of his prosperity how could his descendants hope to guess? Randal silently saluted the old devil, then dragged his attention back to the matter in hand.

'One of these girls who wear trousers,' snorted Henry Burns, glaring across the table, his pink face stiff with rage.

His colleagues exchanged discreet glances. Henry's wife was known to be the prime mover of all that happened in their home; a small, compact woman with great energy and an immovable will.

'She's trying to force the price up,' Andrew McAllister said. 'It is obvious.'

'Is it?'

Randal spoke now for the first time, his voice soft. They all looked at him, waiting for him to speak again. Everyone always looked at Randal Saxton in that way—attentive, deferential, ready to be charmed or convinced depending on the circumstances. He was accustomed to it. He even expected it. It was the birthright of a man born to control a mighty industrial empire.

Andrew, when it became clear that Randal was waiting for him to say something in response to that brief, ambiguous question, cleared his throat. 'I think this girl is shrewd enough to see the obvious!' He spoke with a residual Scots accent, rolling his rs.

'What *is* the obvious?' Randal asked very gently.

'That she has us over a barrel,' said Andrew sturdily. 'We must have that site—it's that simple. She's waiting for us to reach our ceiling—or hers, which ever comes first. There has to be a price at which she'll sell.'

Randal studied Andrew's thin sharp features. 'We've offered her a hundred thousand pounds and she still expects more?' The tone was mildly enquiring, yet somehow it made the other man flush.

'With respect, Randal, we'll pay more,' he retorted. 'I don't need to remind you that that house of hers is right in the middle of our development. We've already spent millions acquiring the rest of the sites and clearing them. She knows we have no choice but to pay her price.'

'You're absolutely convinced it's only a question of price?'

Andrew looked at Randal in astonishment, then sneered, his thin upper lip lifting at the corner. 'You don't believe this newspaper publicity, do you? I've met this girl. She's clever, she's quick—quite clever enough to use the media for her own ends.'

Randal looked at the folder placed in front of him

on the table. He did not open it. He knew the contents by heart.

'Marcia Campion is eighteen. She inherited this house from an aunt a few weeks ago, and we immediately renewed the offer we'd made to her aunt.'

'A very generous offer,' Andrew snapped. 'Seventy thousand pounds for a ramshackle old house in a dockland area of London! It was a windfall for a girl like that. She must have thought it was Christmas.'

Randal quietly went on, 'She rejected our offer and informed us that she intended to turn the house and garden into a communal centre for the neighbourhood.'

'Local agitators gave her that idea,' said Andrew. 'Sentimental nonsense. Jobs are what they need in that area, especially with unemployment running at that level. This girl saw her chance of holding us to ransom, and she took it. The house is an eyesore, a great Victorian eyesore. The garden is a wilderness. The way the press have been talking, you'd think we wanted to pull down some great stately home!'

'It's the oldest building in that borough,' murmured a small, white-haired man from the far end of the table. Heads swivelled to stare at him as though he had committed an act of treachery. He flushed, defensively. 'And it isn't Victorian, you know—it was built in 1815 by a Spitalfields silk merchant and has been in the family ever since.'

'It's more than a house, it's a heritage,' said Randal thoughtfully.

They stared at him in silent, baffled disbelief, and he laughed. 'According to the *Gazette*! I was quoting their leader. They waxed poetic on the subject. We're cast as the big bad wolf with Miss Campion as Little Red Riding Hood.'

'There was a picture of her in today's *Post*,' said Henry, pulling a newspaper out of his briefcase and flinging it angrily into the centre of the table. It lay there, crumpled and untidy. Randal leaned forward and opened it. Out of the grey pages stared a face which, even in this appalling reproduction, was startlingly alive; heart-shaped, with wide-set smiling eyes and a tenderly shaped mouth which had a natural curve of joy to it.

'My God! No wonder we've been getting a bad press. She's a gift to them,' Randal breathed.

The six men stared at the picture, each face mirroring a strong reaction, ranging from delight to rage. Andrew coughed angrily. He resented the charm of her features as much as the obstinacy of her will.

'The longer all this takes the more it's going to cost us. Don't forget, we have a contractor's deadline to meet. We have to get that site cleared and the building up as soon as possible. We've borrowed to cover our costs and each extra day adds to the interest we shall have to pay. We have to break the deadlock somehow.'

The argument burst out again. They had already spent hours discussing it and they were going round in circles, getting as irritated with each other as with Marcia Campion.

Randal suddenly cut across their voices. He never needed to raise his clear, unemphatic tone. 'I'll go and see her myself,' he said.

The flat statement stopped them dead. They stared at him.

Andrew looked alarmed. 'I wouldn't advise that, Randal,' he said.

Andrew was afraid that Randal would take over the negotiations. He was always resentful when anyone else showed an interest in his particular field of management. It was unusual for Randal to do so. He both proclaimed and practised delegation of responsibility. His father, the late Howard Saxton, had frequently told him that management was a genius for doing nothing but tell other people what to do. Randal had been born with this genius. That it also entailed an ability to note, and stop, time-wasting activity; to streamline work patterns and evolve more productive routines, often escaped less able minds, who merely saw him in his carefully nurtured public image of the playboy-millionaire. Randal had always found it extremely useful to cultivate this image. Opponents were misled into imagining that he was a lightweight fool who could be treated with contempt, and by underestimating him were themselves defeated in sudden brilliant unexpected battle.

His colleagues on the board knew him better by now. They saw the toughness of the bone structure under his good looks; the ruthless coldness of the vivid blue eyes, the jut of that angular, stubborn jaw and the tight, strong mouth.

Some people had even noted an elusive resemblance to the stormy founder of the firm, James Saxton; a look of menace now and then about the eyes, a dangerous twist of the firm lips. The twentieth century, as Randal's cousin Perry had once observed, had *its* fair share of pirates, even if they no longer carried cutlasses or sailed the seven seas in search of prey.

Randal looked at Andrew now, his eyes sharp. 'You've had weeks in which to conclude this negotiation, Andrew. Time I took a hand, I think.'

Henry Burns laughed. It amused him to see Andrew lose face, to hear, beneath Randal's cool tones, the crack of the whip. 'I agree,' he said. 'You'll have her eating out of your hand in ten minutes flat, by previous records.'

The others laughed. It would not be the first time Randal had used his undoubted attraction as a business weapon against a member of the opposite sex.

'Then that's settled,' said Randal, leaning back in a gesture of dismissal.

When they were leaving the boardroom a few moments later Andrew casually enquired, 'How's Lady Tarreton, by the way?'

Randal's eyes lifted in icy comprehension. He knew that Andrew was taking an oblique revenge for having had the negotiations taken out of his control. Andrew knew that such small failures were significant in this dog-eat-dog world. He resented Randal's intervention and was, in any case, secretly hostile to him. Andrew had fought his way up the business ladder from the bottom. Randal had been born into his power, and Andrew could never forget it.

Isobel Tarreton, the widow of a shipping magnate, had earlier resisted an attempted merger between her firm and Saxton's, only to change her mind after Randal had exerted a little of his charm. Their names had been coupled in the public mind ever since, but the affaire had never progressed.

Andrew had wondered, even secretly hoped, that Randal would at last have to pay the price for his ruthless use of the personal in business. Isobel Tarreton had seemed almost as determined as Randal himself. Gossip columnists had hinted at a forthcoming marriage. Isobel's friends had chosen their hats. But Randal had, somehow, remained elusive.

There was only one constant feminine presence in Randal's life—the only feminine member of Saxton's board, Julia Hume, who had progressed from acting as their legal expert on company law to her own place on the board in four years, partly due to Randal's influence, partly to her own cool intelligence and grasp of affairs.

Andrew, along with the rest of their acquaintance, had often pondered curiously upon this discreet, and puzzling, relationship. Clearly they saw a great deal of each other, both in and out of business hours. Clearly there was considerable intimacy between them—ten minutes in their company made that clear. But how much else there was to know was obscured by their ability to conceal their emotions.

Julia was, at present, abroad on company affairs.

Randal's cold glance made Andrew pale, regretting that he had permitted his malice to show.

'Lady Tarreton?' Randal looked blandly bored. 'I have no idea.'

'Watch yourself with this girl,' Andrew said roughly. 'She may be just a kid, but she's shrewder than she looks.'

Randal nodded. 'I'll play it by ear.'

The other man remained nervous. 'Perhaps I should come along with you,' he said.

'Andrew, I don't need anyone holding my hand,' Randal drawled, looking at him thoughtfully.

'Of course not, but . . .' There was sweat on Andrew's forehead along the ragged line of his brows. Randal's cool glance noted it, shrewdly. Why was Andrew so nervous about this business?

'But nothing,' he said. 'I'll deal with it alone.'

Andrew swallowed, but was silent. When Randal had left, Andrew hurried to his own light, airy office and picked up the white plastic telephone on his excessively neat desk. He dialled a number and then said abruptly into the receiver, 'Hello? Saxton's coming along there himself. Watch it. Do you understand? Just watch it.' Then he slammed the receiver down with a crash that almost shattered it.

Russell Gold was having the time of his life. He brought his flock of fellow reporters down the long line of kids like a sheepdog hustling sheep, pointing out newsworthy faces with all the fluency of a lifelong resident.

'Dost Mohammed. His dad runs the corner shop. He plays on the pavement—not even a back yard for him because his dad has to use the yard for storage . . .'

Dost, tiny, bright-eyed, grinning, posed for his photograph. Behind him Wesley Stephens danced up and down, eager to appear in the newspapers. His banana grin and curly head drew attention. Wesley

had enough energy and spirit for two, learning so fast
that his mother often watched him with a baffled
mixture of despair and pride. His father was in prison
for two years, of which he'd served half. Josiah
Stephens, impulsive and hot-tempered, had been
caught snatching fur coats from an unguarded
furrier's van during a delivery. In a panic he had
punched the furrier, breaking his jaw, then hidden,
childishly, in his own house, where the police found
him two hours later. Josiah had wept in court as he
was taken down to begin his sentence. His wife had
wept often since. Marcy Campion, watching, thought:
Wesley is a genius. But what is he learning? The waste
of it all made her feel sick.

Russell came back looking flushed and excited.
Tall, very dark, with gleaming white teeth and liquid,
pleading eyes, he had been one of her keenest sup-
porters from the first, yet she was secretly doubtful of
him. Was he genuinely concerned about the playground, the community centre, or was he only using
the situation to make money and a name for himself?
She hated to feel distrust towards people, but she had
already begun to be wary.

'They want another one of you, darling, with
young Wesley. Now, remember! No smile. They want
a wistful expression . . .'

'Do I have to?' She was sick of the publicity, the
fuss, the anonymous letters and stupid patronising
questions.

'This is the way things get done,' Russell assured
her. 'You want to beat the big boys, don't you?'

The photographers looked at her like fishmongers

regarding the blue-grey slippery piles of herring on their slabs. 'This way, darling! Turn your head to me, love . . . Hey, miss!'

Marcy looked at them defiantly, chin up, her fine mop of ringleted, marmalade-coloured hair blowing in the wind, her slanting, bottle-green eyes glinting in the sunlight. Eighteen years old, she had been brought up in the wild fastness of Cornwall, in an elegant old house built above a lashing sea, by parents who were already middle-aged when she was born and had never been quite sure how to treat the tiny, squawling scrap with which life had presented them. Marcy had learnt to run head-on into the wind, to fight the elements with all her fierce energy, and to be as wary as a wild animal of the scholarly, elegant home her parents had made. She loved her mother and father, but she felt remote from them, and when they died, soon after her seventeenth birthday, she had already learnt to live alone.

Shortly afterwards her aunt Thomasina had died, leaving her the old London house, the family springboard from which the Campions had spread out over the world. There were uncles in various parts of the Commonwealth. Cousins in Hong Kong and Jamaica. An aunt in Canada. Marcy knew nothing much of any of them; they were not a communicative family. Aunt Thomasina had left the old house to Marcy for no reason at all—almost as if she had picked the girl out of a hat.

Marcy had been excited by the news. Her own house in Cornwall was leasehold—the lease had another year to run, that was all, and she had been considering leaving the West. Now she knew she would go to London, and she made rapid preparations.

Her aunt's solicitor was a thin, grey, weary man. He looked at the girl indifferently, gave her the keys and informed her of the 'very handsome' offer for the property.

'You can sign the papers today,' he ended drily.

'Seventy thousand pounds!' Marcy was hoarse with amazement. 'Did you say seventy . . .'

He nodded. 'It's completely ridiculous, of course—the land is worth very little intrinsically. But the developers want to acquire your property in order to complete their plans.'

'Developers?' Marcy gazed at him. 'You mean they want to pull the house down?'

He nodded again, his neck wrinkling like the neck of some thin, aged tortoise, in grey folds. 'Saxton and Company. They plan to build across the whole block. The development is to be vast, I understand.'

Marcy had put aside the idea for the moment, staggering though the figure of seventy thousand pounds seemed to her. She had been eagerly waiting to see the house. She knew something of her family history, although her parents had not discussed it much. That the family had once lived in Spitalfields during the eighteenth century she knew, and that they had prospered, and built this house in the newly developing marsh area along the river which was later to become the dockland areas of London. She had a vague yet eager curiosity about the house.

When she first saw it she thought that there had

been some mistake, but then she looked again at the
name on the corner of the road. Paradise Street.

The house stood in a vista of corrugated iron
fences, broken pavements and dirty wisps of paper
blowing desultorily along the filthy road. There were
no buildings apart from the house itself.

All around rose high flats, like concrete mountains
looking down upon a grimy valley.

At the other end of Paradise Street a narrow alley
intersected, choked with workmen's cottages and
shabby shops with peeling paint, cracked wood and
uneven roofs.

A fence had been erected around the site of the old
house and she could not find an opening. She saw the
upper storey over the top of the fence—a flat
Georgian façade with a stark elegance born of func-
tional lines and generosity of proportion. The dusty
windows seemed to appeal to her mournfully against
the dull sky.

She went to the council offices and requested them
to open up the site again. They seemed taken aback
to find her determined. The Borough Surveyor, a
choleric gentleman of fifty in a rough liver-striped
tweed, seemed almost disposed to refuse to comply,
but Marcy, despite her youth, was aware of her
rights.

'You had no business fencing off private property,'
she reminded him.

He grunted furiously about protecting property,
and then asked abruptly if she had not heard the offer
from Saxton's. 'Is there any point in opening the site?
You'll be selling, anyway.'

'I haven't decided,' she said.

'Not decided? What does your father say about that, young lady?' he asked, half angry, half patronising.

'He's dead,' she told him.

He flushed. 'Oh.' He cleared his throat. 'Your guardian?' He laughed half-heartedly. 'You can't be of age yet, I fancy.'

'I'm of age,' she assured him. 'Will you have the fence opened?'

He gave in with reluctance.

As she was about to leave she asked idly what sort of redevelopment scheme was scheduled to begin on the cleared site. 'Flats? Or houses?'

'An office block with shops below,' she was told curtly.

She had looked at him in appalled disbelief. 'An office block? Have you seen those streets? Those people need houses. Homes, a park, anything to make up for that inhuman landscape.'

She had met a stone wall of indifference. The plans had been approved. Saxton's, the multi-national company, intended to build a vast complex on the site for commercial and private use.

'People need shops. They need work.' The Borough Surveyor had been briefly patronising. 'Things are never as simple as you young people think!'

As she left Marcy had heard him pick up the telephone and dial. Looking back her eyes met his, and she saw hostility in his glance.

Marcy had gone back to Paradise Street with a council workman who had crossly wrenched out the nails and lifted out two boards so that she could walk on to her property.

It was, she found, quite a large area—oblong in shape, with a red brick path running between a jungle of shoulder-high grass, towards the grimy walls of the house, against which grew a lilac tree in brilliant green leaf. There were, too, several very old apple trees, mossy and gnarled, like sulky old men, creaking in the wind, their leaves coated with dust.

The workman, a West Indian with big ears and a close-cropped head, came inside after her and looked slowly around. A light suddenly lit his sulky face. 'Nice little piece of land here, miss,' he said. 'You could grow stuff here, that's for sure . . .' He began to pace about, kicking at the dark, sour soil. 'Yeah, if you was to put a bit of goodness back into this earth you could grow vegetables here.'

'Those trees look dead,' she said.

He studied them, wrinkling his wide nostrils. 'Yeah, they is in a bad way. I'd have them out and plant two young ones . . .' Then he sighed. 'If they wasn't going to build here, that is.'

Something moved at the edge of the iron fence. Out of the corner of her eye she saw a red sweater topped by a small, dark face. She pretended to be unaware of the new arrival and soon he sidled in, crouching in the long grass like a tiger, peering around the summer-bleached stalks at them.

Marcy had a bag of sherbet lemons in her denim jacket. She pulled it out and offered it to the workman. He took one absently, then grinned at her, his whole face coming alive.

'Thank you, miss. You with the council?'

She liked his voice, the warm, lilting rhythms of his speech, her trained ear picking it up instinctively and trying to reproduce it. She had intended to take up a scholarship at a London drama school this year—she had been studying speech and drama privately for some years at home, and wanted to teach it herself, in time. In the autumn, if she had made up her mind, her place would be waiting for her.

'I'm a student,' she told the workman. 'My aunt left me this house, so I came to look at it. They say I should sell it to the developers.'

He grimaced. 'They build on every little bit of land they can. Soon there going to be no land for people to walk on anywhere in this city.'

She was struck by his words and stared at him, then looked up at the high-rise flats, the grey sky behind.

The watcher in the long grass crept closer. Behind him another child had appeared, stalking patiently on all fours.

'My kids play around dustbins all day. Where else they got?' the workman sighed in resignation.

The children were very close now. Marcy turned slowly, grinning, holding out her bag of sweets. 'Want one?'

They froze, staring at her through their screen of pale grass. Then the first, his grin splitting his face, laughed and stood up, taking a sweet with a dive of eagerness.

'Scat, you damn kids!' the workman shouted.

They poised for flight.

'Let them play,' said Marcy. She looked at them, her face heart-shaped, like a child herself in her denims, her hair bright as spilled orange marmalade.

The two boys looked at her, looked at each other. Then they looked around the garden. A strangled whoop came from the throat of the older. He ran, skipping and leaping in ecstatic elation.

The other one turned and vanished, too, in the direction of the hole in the fence.

The workman gave her a frown, a shake of the head. 'That was a silly thing to do, miss. They'll cause bother now.'

'You'd rather they played around dustbins?'

He thought. 'I got to nail that fence back before we go,' he said slowly.

'This land belongs to me, not the council,' she said. 'Leave it open.'

He looked alarmed. 'I got orders to close it,' he repeated.

'They can't give orders about my property,' she said cheerfully.

'I'll have to go back to the Town Hall,' he said. 'I don't know what Mr Askew's gonna say.'

She smiled, offering him her small hand. 'No hard feelings? I'm Marcy Campion, by the way. What's your name?'

He swallowed her hand into his own large dark one, shook it in a firm, friendly fashion. 'I'm Luke Green.'

'You live around here, Luke?'

'Albert Street,' he said. 'I share a house with my brother Ignatius. He lives upstairs, I live down.'

'Albert Street?'

He pointed to the bisecting road. 'That's Albert Street. See the shop on the corner? Next to that there's Crancy Alley. That's a real fleapit.' He gave her a thoughtful look. 'This ain't exactly the West End, you know, miss.'

'Marcy, please,' she prompted.

He stared down at her. The bottle-green eyes twinkled. Luke began to laugh, his teeth big and white.

'A minute ago I was sorry for you, Marcy. Now I'm sorry for Mr Askew. He don't know what's about to hit him.' He turned to go, then halted in dismay, seeing children slipping into the grass in an increasing throng. 'Boy, have you got problems,' he said. 'You don't know what you've started.' Suddenly his jaw clenched as two little girls in bright cotton dresses and spotless white socks came running towards him.

'Papa!' they shouted. 'Is it true? Can we play here?'

'My goodness, Teresa Green, Agnes Green, what are you doing in here? Does your mama know you're here? You get off back home there at once!' His voice was stern, his face frowning.

Marcy saw the two little faces cloud over, the bright eyes grow wet with tears. She looked at Luke reproachfully. 'Is it to be dustbins for ever, Luke? Let them stay for a while. I'll keep an eye on them.'

Luke groaned. 'I hope I don't lose my job over this.' He looked down at the two small girls. Their round eyes begged silently, and he groaned again. 'O.K., O.K. But you go on home and tell your mama where you are, first, and tell her I said it was fine for you to play here a while.'

They were gone, like eager puppies, scampering through the grass. Luke followed them, whistling softly to himself, plucking a blade of grass and chewing on it as he went.

Marcy walked over to the apple trees. A little band of Tarzans already swung from the branches. 'Hi,' she said. 'Anyone know where we could get some rope or an old tyre for a swing?'

'I do,' one said, while the others looked at her warily. 'Down the bottom of Crancy Alley there's a dump.'

'Could you fetch something?' she asked.

A couple of the boys ran off, the others kept watching her, like stray cats ready to fly at the first hint of danger. She looked round at their faces, smiling. 'Did you know my aunt?' She told them her name.

'I'm Wesley,' said the first boy who had arrived. His grin was warming. 'My mum runs the laundrette in Albert Street.'

A Pakistani boy shouted, 'Show-off, show-off!' A fight started, bodies rolling over and over in the dust and grass.

Wesley sat up, triumphant. 'Your aunty was a witch,' he told Marcy.

The others giggled and pushed each other. Marcy stared at them. 'A what?'

'A witch,' Wesley nodded. 'We used to creep in and watch her through that window . . .' pointing at the ground floor of the house. 'Stirring a black pot over the fire . . . witches do that.'

Marcy turned and made towards the house, accompanied by a band of eager, talkative children, all bursting now to tell her their version of Aunt Thomasina.

She unlocked the dusty front door. The key grated in the lock, the hinges protested and squeaked as the door swung slowly back. The children crouched, half afraid, half curious, and stared past her into the wide-ceilinged hall.

The still-beautiful fanlight made an exquisite pattern of sunlight on the grimy tiled floor of the hall. There was a vista of doors set in a long wall from which ancient wallpaper peeled damply. Slowly the little party advanced.

They turned in at the first doorway on the left and found themselves in the room in which, according to the children, the old lady had mainly lived in her last years.

Here, too, the paper peeled from the walls, in sagging strings. The room was elegant in proportion, with high light windows, and a high ceiling. The fireplace was exquisite—moulded in cream-painted panels, with an ironwork grate above which swung a round hob.

'That's what she cooked on,' Wesley pointed. A saucepan stood on the tiled hearth, blackened by fire.

Marcy felt tears prick at her eyes. She had a vision of the old lady, alone and cold, in this great chill house, cooking some inedible meal in a saucepan.

A sagging bed stood on the other side of the room. Had Aunt Thomasina died in it? Marcy wondered.

Had her last hours been spent in this grey, damp room, spotted with mould and hissing with the spit of rain on the open fire?

She shivered. 'Let's look at the rest of the house,' she said, trying to inject some gaiety back into the proceedings.

Shouting, peering, chattering, they made their way around the house from the attics, in their empty, dusty silence to the great, whitewashed brick cellars, draped with cobwebs and mouse-droppings.

Most of the rooms were furnished, in some fashion, but the furniture was all mildewed, dusty and beyond repair. Mice had made nests in velvet sofas, the horse-hair stuffing of chairs drifted across the floors in little piles, there were broken objects everywhere.

'Change and decay in all around I see,' murmured Marcy to herself.

'Gloomy, ain't it,' Wesley agreed, shuddering dramatically.

When they emerged into the daylight they found a work party busy building an obstacle course with old tyres, planks of rotten wood and piles of bricks—the tyres swung from the trees, the planks were raised on heaps of rubble and brick. The whole garden was filled with children, playing and working with vigour and noisy enthusiasm.

A little crowd of women were standing at the opening in the fence. Marcy took a deep breath and walked over to them.

They looked at her suspiciously.

She smiled and began to talk. Soon she was sitting on an orange box, a mug of tea in her hand, listening as the women talked about the new development.

A sleek car drew up. Mr Askew, the Borough Surveyor, climbed out, greeted with a hail of catcalls. He glared at Marcy.

'There's some tea left in the pot,' she said cheerfully. 'Would you like a mug?'

'What do you think you're playing at?' he retorted, ignoring her offer. 'You can get those kids out of there double quick. This fence has to be nailed up again. You're breaking the law.'

'What law?' she asked.

The children stopped playing and came slowly over to listen. The women stood with folded arms, staring at him.

'I'm not going to argue with you,' he blustered. 'Just get those kids out of there. You've got no right . . .'

'No,' she said. 'You're the one who has no right— no right at all to nail a fence around my property. This is private property and I demand that you take down that fence.'

The children began to dance like dervishes, whooping and grinning.

Mr Askew went dark red. 'Don't you talk to me like that, miss!'

'I'm sorry,' she said. 'I don't mean to sound rude, but I will not allow you to dictate to me. I have decided to give this land to the community—the house will make a fine community centre, and the garden will make a wonderful playground for the children.'

'You can't do that!' he gasped.

'Why not?' she asked simply.

'Saxton's want this land,' he said.

'They can't have it.'

'You don't understand,' he said thickly. 'This land is in the centre of the whole scheme—they've got to have it or the rest of the project will be impossible.'

'The people here need somewhere to go,' she said softly. 'A house with many big rooms where they can play table tennis, put on plays, have jumble sales or coffee mornings. A house where their children can play safely in the fresh air . . .'

The women nodded, sighing. The children watched him. Mr Askew perspired and wiped his forehead. 'Jobs,' he mumbled. 'Fine shops . . . offices.' The watchful faces did not soften.

He retreated, leaving the garden unfenced. Wesley dragged a woman from the fence, holding her plump hand tightly. 'Marcy, this is my mam.'

'How do you do, Mrs Stephens?' said Marcy, smiling, holding out her hand.

'Marcy needs somewhere to live, Mam,' Wesley said, looking up at his pretty, smiling mother with appeal.

Mrs Stephens gave Marcy a beam. 'You're welcome to sleep with us. We got a good flat over the launderette—two rooms for sleeping.'

Through the crowd pushed a dark young man. 'I'm from the local paper,' he told her. 'Could I have a chat? What's going on? Is it true you're refusing to sell the house? You're giving it to the council for a community centre?'

She nodded. 'I've offered it to them, yes. They don't

seem to be very keen so far.' She grinned at him. 'I expect you know Mr Askew.'

He winked. 'Like my own brother! And, strictly off the record, did you know that Askew's cousin is one of the sub-contractors for the project here? He's doing the electrical side, or some of it. Saxtons have a number of local contractors signed up to work on this project. That's how they got the scheme through the planning stage so easily. Half the council have some sort of interest in seeing the work go ahead.'

Marcy was horrified. 'But that's corrupt!'

He grinned easily. 'You obviously don't understand how local government works. Look, most of those on the council are either local businessmen or professionals like teachers or accountants. They're interested in politics. They join the local parties, get elected to serve a term on the council. They go on doing their usual jobs. How do you separate council business from self-interest in that case? If a contract comes up, why shouldn't they apply? There's no evidence that the contracts weren't tendered for in the usual way, quite openly. There was no direct corruption. It's all very much a nod and a wink.'

'But Mr Askew is employed by the council,' she protested.

'I don't say Askew himself has any reason for wanting the scheme to go through. Just that his cousin has a reason.' He gazed at her. 'You need advice. The council aren't going to accept your offer. They'll wriggle out of it somehow.'

'Advice?' she asked dubiously.

'A solicitor,' he said.

'I can't afford one,' she said.

'My brother Sim will help,' Russell told her.

He brought Sim down to the house later that afternoon. 'It will be a pleasure,' Sim told her. 'I grew up in this human desert.' He looked around the garden, at the boys, hanging upside down like two-toed sloths from the apple trees; at the little girls seated demurely in makeshift houses fashioned from orange boxes, pouring imaginary tea from broken-spouted old teapots, or dressing dollies with flowers, while the work-party continued to build their ever-more-ambitious obstacle course around the garden. 'I wish I'd had a place like this to come to,' he said.

Sim was very elegant, his dark hair silvering at the temples, his lantern-jawed face wistful. 'You like kids?' The question was a sigh.

Later Russell told her, 'Sim's wife Lisa won't have any kids. She has her career to think of . . .' He put a hand on his hip, assumed a haughty expression and sauntered up and down looking swan-like. 'Lisa is a model. You should hear what my mother has to say about Lisa! Mum had eight kids, five boys, three girls. Two of the girls died, one of the boys. So far none of the rest of us has provided Mum with what she thinks a Jewish mother has the right to expect! You ever seen a frustrated granny? Come and meet my mother. She suffers every time she sees a pram in the street. She'll make you weep with sympathy.' He gazed at her, looking suddenly anguished and furious at the same time.

Russell had a gift for conveying character in a few words, acting the part of the people he talked about, making them come alive with a gesture, a look.

He came with Lisa one morning, showing her the child-infested garden. Lisa looked at Marcy with slanting, dark, hostile eyes and kept her at a distance.

Russell went to see the council with Marcy. They had gathered in a high-ceilinged council room to see her. They pleaded, argued, descended to threats, but Marcy was firm.

'They were all against me,' she said later to Russell.

'That was only a committee,' he told her lightly. 'Wait until the full council debates your offer. Then we'll see fireworks. Our editorial will come out before the meeting. The left will swing to your side—wait and see. Meanwhile, I'm trying to get the telly people interested.'

The television cameras came down to film next day. They were there all day, but that night there was only two or three minutes of film shown. Wesley's banana grin and Marcy's vitality made an impact all the same. Letters and offers of help began to pour in—she found herself famous overnight, the house besieged by journalists.

The council meeting was set for a date on the following week. Russell and Sim assured her that the council was deeply divided over the issue. If they accepted her offer, they would have to finance the upkeep of the house and playground for ever. If they turned her down and she sold to Saxton's, it would be unpopular with the local people, but the businessmen of the borough would be delighted.

'You can see their dilemma,' Sim said reasonably. Their picketing of the Town Hall had been highly publicised. Russell seemed ecstatic over it, but Marcy felt unhappy. The simple issue of a place for children to play had become clouded in her mind. She hated the stares, the newspaper stories, the television cameras. She was delighted when, after an hour or two, she found herself at last alone in the garden. The children were at school. The summer holidays had not yet begun. For a while she had the house and garden to herself.

When Randal Saxton walked in among the bleached grass he found her hanging from a branch of one of the apple trees by one hand, trying to tie a knot in a rope with the other, her jeans-clad legs hitched around a rubber tyre for support.

She looked down as he came to stand below her. Their eyes met obliquely through the crook of her arm.

She saw a striking man of thirty or so, crisp dark hair faintly tinged with silver, blue eyes glinting up at her in sunlight, features sculpted in austere lines like a crusader on a tomb, until he smiled, when his eyes danced in mockery and he seemed a totally different man.

He saw a grubby ragamuffin with a tousled, wind-swept mop of bright hair and a curling, triangular smile.

Taken off guard, she unwarily let go and fell. He caught her as she did, tumbling backwards at the impact, and they rolled over on the grass. For a moment, he was quite winded.

Then he opened his eyes. She·sat up, away from him, and began to laugh.

Behind her head the sun dazzled like a halo, turning her hair to fiery gold. Randal stared, feeling as if his eyes were stretching to their limit.

He had a curious, flashing image of a picture from an old fairy story book; his favourite when he was a boy. There had been a princess seated in a garden looking at a green frog which held a golden ball in its mouth. The princess had had golden curls and a radiant, heart-shaped face.

'Have I crushed your ribs to smithereens?' she asked, giggling.

He didn't answer. He couldn't. He was afraid to speak. A breathless excitement held him in a spell, and he had to fight against an impulse which amazed and terrified him—a desire to grab her by her thin shoulders and kiss her ruthlessly.

'Do say something,' she begged, faltering. 'You haven't really broken something, have you?'

He forced a smile. Somehow his lips parted and words came from his tongue. 'No, of course not. I'm just flattened a bit, that's all.'

She laughed. 'You aren't a reporter, are you?' looking at his extremely elegant, well-cut suit, his air of authority. 'Or from the council?'

'Neither,' he assured her. 'My name is Randal . . .'

'Well, Mr Randal,' she interrupted before he had finished, 'What are you doing here?'

He looked at her in dumbfounded silence, then on another wild impulse, he said, 'I wondered if I could help in any way.'

'Help?' She smiled. 'Well, that's very kind, but there isn't much you could do at present, Mr Randal.'

'I could buy you lunch,' he said lightly.

She looked taken aback, then grinned. 'Why should you?'

'Well, you could buy me one,' he said. 'After all, you did almost crush me to smithereens.'

Marcy looked ruefully at him, turned out her empty pockets. 'I'm stony broke today. You see, my allowance is spent. I get it on the first of the month and this is right at the end.'

'Then let me buy you lunch,' he offered. 'You must eat something.'

'Oh, I've got some bread and some cheese,' she said cheerfully. 'You're welcome to share that.'

'I was thinking of something more substantial,' Randal said with a smile.

'Fish and chips?' Her mouth curved upward. 'Don't tempt me. I adore them.'

Randal hesitated, swallowing. He had been intending to drive her back into the West End to eat at some more customary haunt. Then his blue eyes dwelt on her denims and he grinned. 'Come along, Eve,' he said. 'Let the serpent tempt you with a plate of fish and chips.'

He had parked his car discreetly in the Town Hall car park. They walked along Albert Street, therefore, to the fish and chip shop at the far end, where a few tables were set out in the steamy atmosphere. Plastic tablecloths, huge salt shakers and vinegar bottles, fly-blown calendars on the wall . . . Randal stared at them with dismay before he followed her slight figure inside.

They were, as yet, the only customers, and were

served brightly by a young woman with dark red lipstick, dark red nails and a peasant-style dress. Marcy seemed to know her. Randal paid, returning the curious, admiring smile from the young woman with a polite smile of his own. Then they carried their plates to one of the tables.

'Fantastic,' Marcy breathed, gazing at the golden curl of fish. 'I'm ravenous!'

Randal gingerly started to eat and was surprised to find himself enjoying the food. 'Very good,' he said, and received a grin.

'First time you've ever done any slumming?' she asked him bluntly. 'Who are you, really, Mr Randal? What are you really doing down here?'

CHAPTER TWO

'MORE to the point,' he said gravely, 'who are you? Who gives you your allowance, and are you really living in that decaying mausoleum?'

Marcy liberally salted her chips with one of the huge shakers. Her green eyes twinkled at him over the table. 'I noted the change of subject,' she said. 'We'll get back to you later. As for my allowance, it comes from my father.' She ate a chip. 'Who is dead,' she added regretfully.

'I'm sorry. Were you very close?'

She shook her head. 'Worse—very distant. We both meant well, which makes it sad, don't you think? That we never got closer than shouting distance, I mean? He was so old for a father, and he didn't begin to understand our generation. He wanted to love me, I'm sure of that, but there was all that between us . . . half a century of life for him, and things had all changed so much without his ever understanding why.'

'Your mother?'

She sighed again. 'The same. She was forty-three when I was born. They died in a car crash, together, last year.'

'What other family have you got?' Randal watched her over the table with half-closed eyes that traced the bright fall of hair from her pale forehead, the tender

36

pink mouth, the surprisingly determined jawline.

'None,' she said. The sound had a poignant ring. She was clearly aware of it, for she lifted her eyes to his face with a little shake of her shoulders, as if forcing herself out of that mood. 'As to why I'm at Campion House, I imagine you know all that—the publicity has been horribly thorough. I think the whole world knows what I eat for breakfast and where I buy my jeans. I never knew reporters could be so tenacious.'

He laughed. 'Like bloodhounds,' he agreed. 'Impossible to shake them off once they're on the scent.'

'Russell tells me I need them, though,' Marcy added wistfully.

'Russell?' He put down his knife and fork, surprised to find that he had eaten his meal to the last crisp golden chip.

'He works on the local paper. He's been very helpful to me since all this started.' Again he caught a definite echo of unspoken feeling and he watched her curiously. How vulnerable and transparent her face looked, he thought, and an unexpected surge of protective sympathy filled him.

'You sound a little doubtful about him,' he observed.

'Do I?' She looked taken aback, then grimaced, her nose wrinkling in a childish, charming gesture. 'Well, I am, as it happens, though I can't imagine how you guessed.' She looked at him, eyes wide. 'Are you psychic?'

'You have a very expressive face,' he told her.

'Really? How alarming! I've never been told that

before, and I don't know that I like it. It makes me feel . . .' she shrugged, lifting her slender shoulders in a violent movement, 'insecure.'

He waited a moment, then pressed her, 'Why are you doubtful about Russell?'

'I'm not sure. I feel guilty, suspecting him . . .'

'Of what?'

'That's just it—I have no reason to suspect him of anything, and even if he has been . . . well, helping me for his own ends, I have no reason to complain, because really, without his help I wouldn't have known where to begin.'

He patiently unravelled this congested remark. 'What ends do you think he has been furthering?'

'His own career, I suppose,' she sighed. 'It's helped him to make his name known in Fleet Street, and Russell is very ambitious.'

'It must have made him a fortune, as well,' murmured Randal. 'The story has had world coverage— you've been defying a multi-national corporation, you know. Other countries have an interest in what's been happening here.'

Marcy glanced at him quickly, her green eyes narrowing. 'You sound very authoritative.'

The cool eyes surveyed her wryly. 'Do I? I've had personal experience in the field.'

'You've come up against Saxton & Company?' Her tone held astonishment. 'How?'

He took his time in replying, his voice careful. 'I'll tell you all about it some time. Go on with what you were saying about this Russell. How about this advice he's been giving you? Has it always been sound?'

Her brow wrinkled in thought. 'Yes. Yes, I think it has.' She gave him a rueful grin. 'The trouble is, I don't know. I'm really very inexperienced at this sort of thing. I don't even know what it is I don't know.'

'Sounds complicated,' he murmured, his mouth denting humorously. 'But at your age that isn't so surprising.'

'Yes, Grandfather,' she said demurely, the bottle-green eyes smiling teasingly at him through those incredible lashes, and he laughed back at her.

'You,' he said softly, 'are a very impudent child,' and knew that her age was something he suddenly resented. Pushing the thought away, because Randal had the ability to concentrate with great tenacity when he wished to do so, he asked, 'Is Russell your chief source of support?'

'Russell and his brother Sim,' she nodded.

'Tell me about Sim,' he invited.

'While I do,' she said cheerfully, apparently not in the least surprised by his catechism, 'do you think we could have another cup of tea? I'm parched.'

He turned to ask for one, but she hissed, 'You'll have to go up and get it. This is strictly self-service.'

Wryly, Randal went up to the counter and returned, slightly flushed, a little taken aback by the ardent glance of the girl who served him. Marcy watched as he carefully placed the cups on the table, her lips curved in an amused smile.

'Sharon really fancies you, doesn't she?' she enquired lightly.

'Is that her name?' Randal asked faintly irritably. 'She's certainly uninhibited.'

Marcy grinned. 'What did she say to you?' She had watched a faint tide of red creep up his neck as Sharon gazed at him.

'She said you were too young for me, and I would find her more satisfactory,' he said, quite deliberately, his blue eyes watching for signs of embarrassment.

Marcy giggled. 'From what I've heard about her, I've no doubt she understates the case,' she said, her eyes dancing.

'You're quite the most peculiar girl I've ever met,' he said with a look of incredulity. 'I think you must have missed her point.'

'I doubt it,' Marcy said cheerfully. 'She's quite nice under all that stuff she slaps on her face, but she calls everything by its proper name. In this district, they do, you know. The language I've heard would have made my mother's hair curl.'

'It doesn't bother you?' A frown crossed his face, making him suddenly as austere as a carved statue.

'No,' she said calmly. 'The people here have a warmth and honesty I respect. That's what I'm fighting for.'

'Which brings us back to Sim,' he said, sipping his tea.

'He's a solicitor,' said Marcy. 'It was his idea to get a preservation order on the house. He roped in the local conservation group—they were as keen as mustard, because, frankly, there isn't much around here worth conserving. Even the air is polluted.'

'Have you ever considered the case from the other side?' he asked quietly.

'I've heard it,' she said flatly. 'Endlessly, from a

long string of hired trouble-shooters from Saxtons. I
suppose you're one of them, Mr Randal?'

Their eyes held over the table. His face was expressionless, the cold blue eyes surveying her in
sudden assessment, as if they were duellists about to
commence fighting.

'In a way,' he admitted, sharply observing her
every fleeting expression.

She nodded, apparently unsurprised. 'I didn't think
you'd just wandered in by chance,' she said coolly.
She drained her cup and stood up. 'Thanks very
much for the fish and chips—I enjoyed them. Tell
your bosses the answer stays the same.' A gleam in
the green eyes caught his breath. 'I'm not to be
seduced even by fish and chips with their best looking
executive.'

He rose, an odd smile on his hard mouth. 'Do you
think I am?' he asked softly. 'I assure you, that was
not why I came.'

'But you haven't told me why you came,' she
pointed out, shrugging her thin shoulders. 'I have to
put my own construction on your arrival.' She moved
out of the fish shop and he followed her.

'Will you have dinner with me tonight?' he
asked as they stood on the windswept, dusty pavement.

'What? Eat like that twice in one day? I'll get fat,'
she retorted lightly.

'I was thinking of somewhere a little more . . .' His
blue glance wandered distastefully over the neighbourhood, the corrugated fences, the peeling paint-
work on the shops, the scraps of paper littering the

road. 'Romantic . . .' he ended, turning back to look at her.

Her brows lifted derisively. 'Romantic, Mr Randal? My God, is seduction on the agenda, after all?' The marmalade curls shook with amusement. 'You tempt me, but no, I'm afraid the strain would be too much for me and I would end up laughing myself sick. When Saxtons want something, they try every avenue, don't they?'

His glance lingered on her heart-shaped face, a curious hardness coming into his eyes. 'Do you know anything about Saxtons, Miss Campion?'

'I've been told enough,' she shrugged. 'A sort of commercial octopus which has tentacles everywhere.' Her eyes mocked him. 'I'm sure you fit in very well there.'

Randal found himself becoming angry, something he rarely did. Andrew had said this girl was quick, he thought. He had come down here with the full intention of using the charm and sex appeal he had often used before in similar circumstances, and to hear himself bluntly described as a commercial octopus somehow got under his skin.

'Seduction was not, and is not, on my agenda, Miss Campion,' he said grimly.

'Good lord, a pompous octopus,' she grinned, beginning to walk away along the street.

Irritably he found himself falling in beside her, although it was clear to him that his chances were diminishing minute by minute.

'I fail to see why you can't have dinner with me,' he said, furious with himself for his inept handling of the situation. 'Or are you afraid you may find yourself giving way, Miss Campion?'

She halted, facing him indignantly, green sparks lashing out at him from the wide eyes. 'I'm not afraid of anything of the sort,' she said, her small chin defiant. 'Just because Sharon fell for you like a ton of bricks it doesn't make you God's gift to women, let me tell you . . .'

'Then there's no reason why you shouldn't have dinner with me,' he said softly.

She stared, her mouth parted in chagrin.

'I'll pick you up at seven at the house,' he said swiftly, seeing he had caught her at a loss for words temporarily. Before Marcy could summon up a stinging refusal he had strode away. She saw him clearly for a second, tall, handsome, marked with that curious distinction. Then he had gone, and she stamped her foot in sudden burning irritation.

When she got back to the house in Paradise Street she found Sim stalking about with a few earnest souls who beamed at her, greeting her eagerly. 'The local conservation lot,' Sim hissed out of the corner of his mouth.

She spent an hour with them, walking around the house, listening to their cries of delight and excitement over what they saw. One of them had a vast leather tome in which he showed her etchings of similar buildings of the same period, sighing over them.

'This house could be a focal point for local community feeling,' he mused.

Marcy glanced out of one of the high windows at

the children at their tireless games in the garden, and thought how much more such freedom was needed. The garden, more than the house, seemed to be what she was fighting for, despite her personal reverence for her family past. Coming from the wild beauty of Cornwall to this unutterably dreary place she had been struck deeply by the lack of space in which children could be free. Formal, tidy municipal parks were intended for activities which were alien to children. She herself as a child had much preferred the rough-hewn caves and rocky pools of the foreshore to the neatness of her own garden.

When the rest of the group had gone, Sim lingered, staring out at the children with wistful eyes.

'Why don't you come to dinner with me and Lisa tonight, Marcy?' he asked at last, turning to her, as if aroused from a sad reverie.

'I've got a date, thank you,' she smiled, inwardly amused by her own phrasing, since her appointment with Mr Randal was not quite so easily described.

Sim surveyed her in a new way. 'I didn't know you had a boy-friend, Marcy?'

She grinned impishly at him. 'That's not quite how I would describe him,' she said.

He cocked a shrewd eyebrow. 'You aren't moving out of your class, I hope? Little girl like you, getting all this publicity, might attract the odd nut.'

'That wouldn't describe him, either,' she said, her mouth lilting into a smile.

'You're very secretive,' said Sim, eyeing her curiously. 'Do I know him?' His eyes widened. 'It isn't Russell, is it?'

'Russell?' She stared at him, then shook her head. 'No, of course not.'

'Why of course not?' Sim asked. 'Russell's a nice boy.'

'Your mother wouldn't approve,' she said lightly. 'She has Michelle lined up for Russell when he finally stops ducking.'

Sim grimaced. 'Russell doesn't seem to know that.'

Marcy smiled gently. 'He knows. He just doesn't want to turn in his running shoes yet.'

Sim laughed, running a hand through his hair. 'You've become one of the family very quickly, Marcy, you know that? My mother likes you.'

'So long as I never become one of the family,' she said in the same gentle tone. 'Your mother likes to make the decisions, and she's already made up Russell's mind for him.'

'She's not always omniscient,' Sim said in sudden dryness. 'She kicks herself every day for letting me marry Lisa.'

Marcy glanced at him softly. 'If I were you, Sim, I'd take Lisa up West tonight and buy her a really extravagant dinner.'

He stared at her. 'Why the hell should I do that?'

Marcy looked at him through her lashes. 'As a sign of penitence,' she said softly.

His face expressed bafflement. 'Penitence for what? I haven't done anything!'

'You've considered it,' she said, her mouth denting.

A flush came into his face. He looked at her oddly. 'What,' he asked carefully, 'are you talking about?'

'I should tell Lisa nothing about it,' Marcy murmured. 'Buy her a dozen red roses, a bottle of French perfume, anything . . . take her to dinner somewhere really stunning, and look as penitent as hell!'

Sim drew a long, shaky breath. 'And what will that achieve?'

'She'll wonder what you've been up to,' said Marcy, opening her eyes wide.

'You can bet on that,' he said grimly.

'She'll possibly even ask you straight out.'

'And what do I say then?'

Marcy's smile was teasing. 'Be reticent,' she murmured. 'Look sheepish.'

'Oh, yeah?' drawled Sim. 'And when she scratches my eyes out?'

Marcy laughed. 'Before she gets that mad, tell her you love her deeply, but you feel you're getting old and you need to have a child.'

Sim crimsoned. He looked away.

'You might hint that there's another woman somewhere who might be prepared to look at things your way . . . but don't go too far along that road, Sim, or she might get really mad. Just let her think you were tempted for a second or two, nothing more.'

'And if I end up in the divorce courts, you'll pay the bill?' he enquired.

'That would never happen in a million years,' she said. 'Lisa has you on a piece of very short string, Sim. All she needs to think is that you've been thinking of straying, and she'll yank you in so fast your feet won't touch the ground.'

Sim gave a grunt of laughter. 'Where do you pick up this language?'

Marcy dimpled. 'I'm a woman. I know what I'd do in Lisa's position.'

Sim glanced at her oddly. 'What made you think I was getting a wandering eye, Marcy?'

She shrugged, her eyes on the window. 'Instinct.'

He put a hand gently to her marmalade curls. 'I must have been more obvious than I realised.'

She flushed, keeping her eyes averted. 'You love Lisa, Sim.'

'Yes,' he agreed, ruffling her curls. His hand slid round her cheek and raised it. Flushed, her eyes alertly wary, she looked at him, ready to back away.

'You're a very pretty, very appealing kid,' Sim said huskily. 'I'm sorry if I embarrassed you.'

She smiled, shaking her head. 'You didn't. I was flattered.'

His grin appeared. 'But scared stiff.'

'You'd better go and buy those red roses,' she said.

He bent and brushed his mouth over hers so quickly it was over before she knew he had moved. 'Thanks, Marcy,' he said, and went.

When he had gone she sighed. Sim's interest in her had been a difficult thing to tackle. Aware that it was largely due to his problems with his wife, she had been sorry for him, and, liking him, had been giving the subject a good deal of thought. She was sure Lisa would react with angry, possessive determination once she began to suspect Sim of looking elsewhere, and she knew enough about Lisa by now to know that even her career did not mean as much to her as her marriage.

While she got ready for dinner with Mr Randal she

thought about Sim, a little flattered, as she had told him, by the way he had been looking at her lately. He was a nice man, and the faint prickle of awareness whenever she was with him had been something that disturbed her. She looked at herself with a wry smile. It was really rather astonishing that someone like Sim should have shown any interest at all in her, she thought. She saw her tousled, vivid mop of hair, her faint dusting of freckles, her lack of sophistication, and she thought wryly of Lisa, soignée as a swan, her model's smile haughty and assured. She should have warned Sim not to let Lisa guess it had been herself he had been looking at like that . . . Lisa would never in a million years be jealous of someone like her.

Still, she thought, smoothing her simple green dress down over her hips, Sim was surely smart enough not to have every detail spelt out for him.

She got a brush and angrily pulled it through her wild curls, trying to put some order into them, but they sprang up ruthlessly once more and she groaned.

She eyed her reflection, her mouth cross, but even a careful application of powder and lipstick failed to make her look anything other than what she was; a thin eighteen-year-old in a childishly plain dress.

Well, she told herself with a grimace, Mr Randal had known what she looked like when he forced the invitation on her! He was lucky she was not turning up in her old jeans.

It was too warm to wear a coat. She walked slowly along the pavement, waiting for him, feeling the evening sun like a benediction on her skin. The garden was still full of children, their voices echoing among the grass in that mysterious way, as if they were wild birds among the garden wilderness, a haunting cry of joy which seemed odd in these dusty streets.

Sim swung suddenly out of his car beside her, a grin on his face. Marcy looked up at him in surprise, blinking exaggeratedly at the elegance of his dark suit, his silvered black hair lifted by the soft summer breeze as he looked down at her.

'I rang Lisa at work,' he told her. 'I'm just off to pick her up. She didn't ask any questions, but when I told her where we were dining she got a very suspicious sound in her voice.'

'Sim,' she said warily, 'don't name any names, will you?'

He winked at her. 'You can say that to a lawyer? Discretion is my middle name.'

'I'll keep my fingers crossed for you,' she said, smiling up at him warmly.

'Just do that,' he said, his hand caressing the slender nape of her neck. 'And if it's a boy I'll call him Mark. A girl . . . Marcy.'

'You're leaping ahead a bit,' she laughed, touched.

'I'm betting on that female intuition of yours,' he said wryly. The hand lingered as if reluctant to leave her neck. 'Marcy . . .'

She felt her colour rise under the impact of his look. 'You'd better hurry, Sim. Lisa will be waiting.'

'Oh, wise young judge,' he mocked, his mouth rueful. He kissed her, still holding her neck, and sighed. 'Last time, Marcy,' he muttered. 'I promise.' Then he got into his car, gave her a wave and vanished.

Still flushed and trembling a little, Marcy turned to find herself under cold observation from a long, steel-blue limousine parked a short way up the kerb. She recognised the occupant with a start, and moved towards him. He leaned over and opened the passenger door. She slid inside and turned to give him a curling smile of derision.

'Company car?'

His face was oddly austere. 'You could call it that,' he said. He ran a chilly look over her, and she wondered if he had expected her to be wearing something more alluring.

Her eyes sparked at him. 'This is the best dress I've got,' she said frankly. 'If it doesn't match wherever you planned to take me, I'm sorry, but as far as I'm concerned the fish and chip shop will be fine.'

'Who was that you were with?' he asked, brushing aside her remark as if it had no importance.

She looked at him in immediate wariness, her flush deepening. 'Sim,' she said flatly.

He frowned. 'The solicitor you told me about?'

She nodded, wondering how much he had seen, how much he had heard.

His hard face observed her. 'A little old for you, isn't he?'

'Not much older than you,' she pointed out softly.

His face tightened. He silently started the car and it purred away down the street, stared at by passers by, swiftly mingling with the other traffic on busier roads as they headed west.

Marcy settled back, enjoying the unusual comfort of the car, eyeing the glittering dashboard with childish interest, bouncing a little on the springy leather of the seats.

Randal glanced at her sideways. 'Sit still,' he ordered, as though she were a little girl.

'Yes, sir,' she murmured, her mouth in that triangular smile he found so oddly attractive. 'Where are you taking me?'

He gave her a glinting look. 'In that dress? God knows. You might just pass as a schoolgirl out for the day, I suppose.'

'You could pretend I was your daughter,' she suggested slyly.

She saw his hands grip the wheel and felt the anger in him. 'One day I'll lose my temper with you, Marcy,' he said softly.

She felt a sudden quiver of mixed apprehension and excitement, as though, playing with a dog she had suddenly discovered it to be a wolf.

She leaned back, assuming a sudden grave air. 'Does the proposition come before dinner or after?' she enquired coolly.

'Proposition?' His brows rose steeply.

'You aren't taking me out to dinner in the West End without some ulterior motive,' she pointed out.

'I thought,' he murmured softly, 'we had agreed my motive was seduction.'

She giggled. 'Not in public, surely?'

He observed her obliquely through his lashes. 'You would prefer somewhere private?'

Marcy was abruptly wary. 'I would prefer it if you turned round and took me straight back home,' she said.

'Then you'd never know exactly what I'm up to,' he pointed out in equal gravity.

'I've a pretty shrewd idea,' she retorted.

'I'm fascinated,' he murmured. 'Are you going to tell me?'

'Saxtons sent you to get me to agree to their terms,' she said flatly. 'I would say you'd been told to pick your own methods: bribery, blackmail or corruption . . . no holds barred.' She looked at him, turning, her arm along the seat, facing him. 'They've already tried bribery and failed. Now comes the attempted corruption.'

'Seduction is a much nicer word,' he offered mildly.

'It comes to the same thing,' she said coolly.

His brow lifted. 'Does it? How wide is your experience of either, Miss Campion?'

She did not rise to the bait. Softly, she said, 'I was brought up on the Cornish coast, Mr Randal. On summer days the sea can be as blue as your eyes, but anyone who knows the coast is well aware of the ugly rocks which lurk beneath those waters.'

He glanced at her in sudden intentness. His glance probed hers sharply. 'Did the rocks stop you from swimming, Miss Campion?'

Her eyes danced in amusement, their green bright as glass. 'I swim like a fish,' she admitted.

'I had a feeling you did,' he said.

She felt a peculiar excitement running over her skin, as though electricity tingled through her, and she eyed him cautiously. He was more dangerous than she had supposed.

He pulled up suddenly in a quiet, elegant street of

Georgian houses whose white façades had been care-fully, lovingly preserved over the years. Marcy looked up at them, then at him, her fine brows quizzical.

'I want to introduce you to someone,' he said.

She sat up very straight, her mouth mutinous. 'I'm not as green as I look, Mr Randal. I'm not going in there.'

He leaned on the steering wheel, studying her calmly. 'Not even to meet the managing director of Saxtons?'

She made a whistling sound, her small mouth pursed. 'Good lord, I must have made quite a dent on that monolithic façade if the big wheel himself wants to meet me!'

A look of dry humour touched his handsome face. 'Yes, I think you can say that.'

She gave him a tomboy grin. 'All right, Mr Errand Boy, take me to your leader!'

If her mockery were intended to deflate him it failed. He gave her another dry look of amusement, and came round to help her out of the car, his hand under her elbow.

They went up the four wide white steps beneath the charming portico which was supported by Corinthian pillars. Randal rapped the polished lion's head sharply once. A moment later the door swung open and a butler gave them both a grave, reverent glance.

'Good evening, Mr Randal, sir,' he observed calmly, standing back. 'Good evening, miss.'

Randal nodded to him and led Marcy, his fingers curled around her slender bare arm, through the long hall, with its polished parquet floor and bowls of bright summer flowers, into an elegantly furnished sitting-room.

She stood, entranced, staring around the room in delight. The walls were papered in a silky pale blue which had a faintly raised fleur-de-lis pattern in the same shade at regular intervals. A delicate gilt mirror hung on one wall. On the other two, apart from the one containing a high window, hung quiet landscapes which she recognised vaguely as being Dutch, their muted colours blending into the soft colours of the room. At the window hung floor-length curtains of dark blue velvet. The carpet was white, the pile so deep she could feel it give beneath her feet like snow.

Randal was watching her heart-shaped, expressive face with acute interest.

She looked at him, smiling her triangular little smile. 'So this is how the other half lives! After Paradise Street it looks as genuine as a plastic daffodil.'

His eyes narrowed, a faintly cruel look in them. She was taken aback by the expression, her own eyes enquiring the reason for his sudden hostility.

The butler came into the room, that bland smile on his face. He was a man in his fifties, a trifle portly, his head bald and pink, his eyes pouched, the formality of his dark clothes dousing the essence of his humanity.

'Is there anything I can get for you, sir?' he asked Randal.

Randal turned a cold face towards him. 'I didn't ring,' he said softly.

The butler bowed his head without a reply and vanished like a genie back into a bottle, so that

Marcy almost expected to see a puff of smoke lingering after him.

She looked at Randal in sudden dislike. 'There was no need to snap at him,' she reproved. 'The poor man was only doing his job. Anyway, I would like to know how much longer we've got to wait for the Great Panjandrum himself?'

Randal moved to a smooth, satinwood table which stood behind the wide blue silk brocade couch, and began silently to pour dark amber sherry into two glasses. The soft light of a white glass table lamp shed pale light around his dark figure.

He moved back towards her, a glass in each hand, and gestured to the couch. 'Sit down, Miss Campion, and be patient,' he said blandly.

Marcy hesitated, then sat down at the end of the couch, accepting the sherry, her eye approving the finely chased glass. Randal sat down beside her, turning, an arm along the back of the couch, to look at her.

She sipped the liquid cautiously, her glance still travelling over the room. Randal's eyes moved with equal curiosity over her slender body in the simple little green dress. Sleeveless, round-necked, almost childish, it could not douse her radiant vitality, and he thought with a faint smile that the very simplicity had a telling effect. His roving eyes strayed to the fine, bright ringlets clustered around her neck, and suddenly he recalled the moment when he had sat in his car and watched as that other man, in his darkly elegant clothes, had curved a possessive hand around that slender throat. His blue eyes darkened in a stab of jealousy. She had not moved away. She had smiled up trustingly at the other man, and he had sat and watched, his hands tightening on the wheel in a spasm of anger which had alarmed him.

When the other man, still caressing her neck, had bent to kiss her raised mouth, Randal had been conscious of a rage so bitter it had taken all his will-power to sit still and watch them.

Watching her now, he wondered exactly how far she was involved with the other, and could not believe she was deeply committed. There was that open, disingenuous look to her face which still held traces of childhood.

He suspected passion was unknown to her. The soft lines of those features said as much, and his body shook with sudden urgency as he contemplated the change in her which passion must make. I must be insane, he told himself. She's almost half my age, a schoolgirl, a tomboy with wild, radical attitudes which would upset my whole way of life. But his blue eyes continued to move over her restlessly as he attempted to get a grip on his usual self-control.

Marcy finished her sherry, placing the glass dubiously on the arm of the couch, and turned back to him in challenge.

'I'm getting hungry, if you aren't,' she said crossly. 'As the Great Panjandrum shows no signs of putting in an appearance, I suggest we leave, either separately or together. I can always get a bus home if you prefer to stay here.'

He leaned over, his hard body turning gracefully, and put his own glass on the table behind them, then turned to reach across her for her glass. As their bodies brushed briefly, she felt his glance up at her like a physical touch, and a faint pink came into her cheeks.

He sat round again and smiled at her, a practised, charming smile to which he got only a cool look.

'I thought you were going to have dinner with me,' he said quietly.

'I've changed my mind,' she said.

'I've ordered a very good meal,' he said.

Her eyes narrowed speculatively. He met her stare coolly.

'Is this your house?' she demanded.

He nodded.

She turned and glanced slowly around the room, then back at him, her face grave.

'Who are you?' she asked.

'I'm Randal Saxton,' he said, watching her carefully.

Her eyes studied him blankly for a long moment. Then she lay back against the brocade cushions, laughing. 'Well, well, well . . . so you aren't the errand boy, after all? You're the Great Panjandrum himself?'

'In person,' he said, his mouth twitching.

She looked at him through her long lashes, mischief in her face. 'And this is the big seduction scene after all?'

'I hate to disappoint a lady,' he murmured, and before she could move the lean body swerved to trap her against the cushions, his long hands framing her surprised face.

Marcy had not seriously expected it. She looked at him, blinking, startled.

Randal appeared to be in no hurry. His fingertips slid softly over the soft skin of her cheeks, as if he were learning all the angles and hollows beneath the flesh. His eyes explored her at close quarters, finding odd rays of leonine gold in the bottle-green eyes, watching the black pupils dilate under his gaze, observing almost casually the slow rise of pink under her skin. He stared at her fine dark brows, at the length of her glinting gold-tipped lashes, at her small, tilted nose, and then finally, with intent absorption, at the tender pink mouth, inspecting it calmly, while it began to quiver in sudden alarm under his gaze.

'If your butler comes in,' she said a little uncertainly, 'he's going to be very embarrassed.'

'He won't come in again,' Randal said coolly.

She gave him a flickering, partially defiant smile. 'Well trained, is he? You bark. He jumps.'

'Shut up,' snapped Randal, lowering his mouth to hers.

Marcy felt a prickle of electric astonishment, her green eyes wide open, staring at the austere features as they descended towards her. Randal's mouth touched hers so softly her lips parted in a sigh of surprise, and then, to her own fury, felt her eyes closing as if by instinct, her slender body yielding as if it had suddenly become plastic under the impact of his kiss. His long hands held her face as if their touch were an elongation of the kiss, his warm palms caressing her face, shaping it, possessing it. For a moment

Marcy was held, hypnotised, by the mastery he was using against her.

Then she violently pulled her head backwards, her eyes opening wide in angry amazement.

'What do you think you're doing?' she asked him in such tones of disgust that a twitch overtook his mouth and he was forced to smile, although his blue eyes were very dark and she could hear him breathing oddly.

'Seducing you,' he returned coolly, sitting back in his seat and smiling at her.

Marcy was flushed and irritable. 'Please,' she said politely, 'don't bother on my account. It would make no difference, anyway. I still refuse to sell you my property.'

'Just possibly,' Randal drawled, 'I'm not after the property you mean.'

Her indignant green eyes spat fire. 'I'd like to go home now, Mr Randal Saxton. I'll make do with beans on toast.'

He caught her wrist as she jumped up and she looked down at his elegant, lounging figure, suddenly seeing it as many others had done in the past, charged with a ruthless menace which meant to enforce its own desires. There was a stubborn jut to his jaw, a darkness in the blue eyes.

'We have a lot to talk about, Marcy,' he said in sudden gravity. 'You'll stay to dinner.'

'No, thank you,' she said, her own face as obstinate as his.

'I think you will when you learn what I have to say,' he told her calmly.

'I'm not interested,' she said, trying to pull her wrist out of the iron grip he had on it.

'Not even if I say you've won?' he asked softly, watching her.

She stood very still, frowning, staring at him. 'Won what? A bottle of free champagne and a night in bed with the Great Panjandrum?' she asked scathingly.

He looked dangerous for a second, then his face smoothed out. 'When the new office block is built it will be built around your land, not over it,' he said clearly.

Marcy stood in astonishment, her eyes open wide. 'Do you mean that?'

He nodded, his mouth satirical. 'One of the talents required for success at the top is the knowledge of when one is beaten,' he said wryly. 'Now, if I give you my word your house and land are safe, will you stay to dinner, Marcy, and talk about what's to be done with them?'

She considered the question gravely. 'You know what I want to be done with them.'

'I know only the press stories,' he said. 'I want to talk to you about the practical details of how the scheme is to be financed.'

'Financed?' she frowned.

'It will need to be kept in good condition,' he said, shrugging. 'My company is prepared to be responsible for the upkeep of the place.'

Marcy looked suspiciously at him. 'Is this a scheme to get hold of it in some devious way?'

He grimaced. 'On my word of honour, it will be kept exactly as you want it . . .' His blue eyes quizzically teased her. 'Do you want me to swear it on the Bible?'

She shook her head. 'No, I trust you, Mr Saxton.'

'Randal,' he corrected.

She hesitated. His eyes watched her shrewdly. After a pause she said slowly, 'Yes, Randal.'

He stood up, his hand sliding to her elbow. 'Then we'll have dinner and talk about it, shall we?'

Allowing him to lead her out of the room, Marcy felt a strange quiver of apprehension. She had won. Had she?

CHAPTER THREE

THE dining-room had the same cool, elegant formality of the room they had just left, and Marcy paused to stare around it, reminded vaguely of her own home as a child.

Randal drew back a straight-legged, shield-backed dining chair whose mahogany had a deep inlaid polish which testified to years of loving care. She ran an admiring finger over the carving which embellished the back. 'Hepplewhite,' she murmured.

He gave her a quick look of surprise. 'Yes,' he admitted. 'You like furniture?'

'My father did.' Her glance ran down the long table, taking in the branched silver candlesticks, the crystal, the silver bowls of exquisitely arranged flowers. Everything looked as if it had been arranged for some elaborate banquet, yet she guessed that this was how it always looked when he sat down to eat, and her glance at him held faint compassion. 'Do you eat here like this even when you're alone?' It must be like living in isolation, she thought.

'I'm rarely on my own,' he said drily.

The butler silently appeared beside her, his head inclined in an attitude of deference, proffering a large silver dish in which a selection of hors d'oeuvres were carefully arranged.

Randal took a damask napkin from the table and

shook it out, laying it across her lap, as if she were a child for whom such attentions were necessary.

When the butler had served them both he departed as softly as he had come. Randal lifted his wine glass, smiling at her. 'To the community project,' he murmured.

Marcy smiled, but sipped the wine a little doubtfully. Although he was treating her with curious indulgence she was not unaware of something behind that bland manner. She had done battle with his giant corporation and beaten them, yet here they were, eating alone together in this silken exclusivity, and every nerve in her being warned her against taking him on his face value.

Looking at him through her gilded lashes in sudden appraisal, she remembered with alarm the way he had kissed her. What was he really up to?

'What are you thinking?' he asked, having watched the expressions flickering across her small, mobile face intently.

'Why you've suddenly changed your mind about getting hold of my house,' she said in her direct way.

'You placed us in an invidious position, little Miss Campion,' he told her softly. 'It's very easy for someone like you to make a large company look absurd, and, quite frankly, we can do without the public image you've been busy projecting for us recently.'

'Mr Askew will be furious when he hears,' she said, drinking some more of the wine. It was sending a not unattractive warmth through her, and she relaxed a little more, her cheeks growing faintly flushed, her eyes as green as polished glass.

Randal raised a sharp brow. 'Askew?'

'The Borough Surveyor.' She drank some more of the wine, barely noting that he had refilled her glass in a quiet movement. Her tongue loosened by the unaccustomed effect, she began to retail to him what Russell and Sim had told her about the convoluted dealings which underpinned the Saxton deal in the borough. Randal watched, listening intently. A hardness came into his blue eyes when she said airily, 'Your Mr McAllister is very thick with Mr Askew, Sim says. Wheeling and dealing, Sim calls it. I said it was corruption, but Russell and Sim said it was just the way the wheels got oiled . . .'

The butler served a delicate course of tender slices of chicken in a creamy vinous sauce on a bed of rice with peppers and slivers of mushroom. Over Marcy's bright, ringleted head the two men glanced at each other. Discreetly the butler replaced the bottle of wine which was finished with another, then vanished again, a slightly anxious look on his bland face. Randal Saxton had entertained many women in his home, but Walters had never known him bring home a child so obviously out of her depth, nor could he comprehend why his master was deliberately plying her with wine which she assuredly could not handle.

'Tell me about your home in Cornwall,' Randal invited, as she savoured the taste of the thick white sauce, her lids half lowered in dreamy delight.

Marcy cheerfully told him about it, hardly aware any longer of the fact that she was doing all the talking, her clear light voice full of loving nostalgia, her expressive face revealing her loneliness as a child, her independence, her early habit of self-preservation.

He was amused to note that, although the wine had made her quite careless of consequences, she showed no sign of becoming actually drunk. Beneath her tomboy frankness there was a strong personal dignity which held beneath the impact of the wine, and he wondered if she had become aware of the effect produced upon her.

She looked at the profiteroles which the butler was offering her with regret, her mouth dimpled. 'Oh, I'd love to, but no, thank you,' she smiled with childish greed.

A faint smile on his bland face, the butler delicately placed one of the small objects in front of her. 'Why not try just one, miss?' he suggested in fatherly tolerance.

Marcy turned a grinning face up at him, her triangular smile and bright eyes entrancing. 'You're tempting me,' she said lightly.

Randal's eyes were fixed on her enchanting profile, a curious hard brightness in his eyes. Walters caught the look and withdrew, more and more perplexed.

Marcy lovingly tasted the profiterole. A sigh came from her. 'Ambrosial,' she remarked. Looking at him, she asked, 'Aren't you having any?'

He shook his head, charm in his face. 'They were intended for you,' he admitted.

'Oh, and I only had one. I'm sorry.'

'Coffee?' he asked her. She watched him add swirls of thick cream which floated in marbled streaks across the coffee.

'I shall never forget this meal,' she said with easy

frankness. 'Do you always eat like this? I've never eaten like it in my life. Who cooks it? Your butler?'

His mouth quirked. 'Walters? He would be shattered by the suggestion. No, I have an extremely good French chef.'

Marcy snorted, coffee going the wrong way. Randal, with a look of concern, patted her on her thin back, and she gradually recovered, but the laughing eyes she turned on him made his brows rise.

'What did I say that was funny?'

'A French chef,' she said. 'You said it so calmly too . . . like someone saying "I've got an elephant in the bathroom".'

Randal lowered his eyes to his coffee. 'I'm a very wealthy man,' he said softly. 'Would you rather I pretended I was not?'

She considered the question soberly. 'No,' she decided, shaking her head. 'Honesty is the best policy.'

'Is it?' he asked, as if he took her words in quite another context. 'Always, would you say?'

She thought oddly of Sim, and a little flush rose into her cheeks. She turned away, sudden constraint in her face. 'It ought to be,' she said on a regretful note.

Randal watched her in abrupt intensity. Why had that strange look come into her mobile face? What had she thought of that made her stop smiling and look grave? He watched her, thinking that every look, every word, of hers was becoming incredibly important to him. He was becoming consumed by a burning desire to know her as he had never known any other human being.

'I ought to be going,' she said, glancing at the lyre-shaped French clock which suddenly chimed on the mantelpiece.

'We haven't talked about our project yet,' he said casually. 'More coffee?'

She was about to refuse when he refilled her cup, then shrugged and accepted it, feeling the queer prickling heat which had invaded her body as she drank the wine seem to recede. The coffee would clear her head, she thought.

'Shall we take it into the sitting-room while Walters clears the table?' he suggested.

Marcy followed him, sinking into the soft depths of the couch with a relaxed sigh. Randal moved softly around, lowering the lights, and she sipped her coffee, a sleepy content on her lowered lids, unaware of what he was doing because she was becoming more and more drowsy.

Randal removed her cup to the satinwood table and sat down beside her. 'My main idea was that we should get a suitable architect to plan a way in which we could involve your house and garden into the actual fabric of our development,' he said quietly.

She was lying back, her heart-shaped face filled with drowsiness. 'I don't follow,' she murmured, trying to grasp what he said.

'No?' said Randal, his long hand pushing back the marmalade ringlets with tender precision until the whole outline of her features could be seen without concealment. 'Your own idea of a local communal centre is the lynch-pin of the scheme,' he said. 'What we have to do is decide the exact nature of the various parts of the centre . . . in other words what the local people would prefer.' His thumb slowly caressed along the smooth pink cheek. 'If we're going to do this in true democratic fashion, an open local meeting would be ideal.'

Marcy was finding it hard to keep her eyes open. 'Mm,' she said, yawning, like a sleepy little kitten, her pink mouth parted to show her neat white teeth.

Randal's voice spoke again, close to her ear. 'Followed by the formation of a committee, either elected at the meeting, or chosen from among various local bodies.' His mouth lightly brushed the delicate outer lobe of her ear. 'Obviously you should be on this committee,' he said, his mouth proceeding to move, with infinitesimal lightness, over her ear and cheek. 'It wouldn't be a bad idea to have Russell and this Sim.' Carefully his lips approached her mouth, oblique, tentative, watching her sleepy face for reaction.

Marcy heard a strange, heavy beat somewhere above her. A clock? she thought dazedly. Forcing her lids, heavy with the weight of yearning for sleep, apart, she found Randal so close her eyes stared into his in surprise. The strange sound she had heard, she deduced after a second or two, was the beating of his heart.

He looked at her in what she considered a very odd fashion. 'Marcy,' he said in sudden huskiness, and his mouth moved with exploratory tenderness against her own. Marcy sighed, her eyes closing again. Her thin arms slid round his neck, and the heavy beating of his heart doubled its pace. He suddenly lifted her up into his arms, pulling her on to his knees, and a flutter of anxiety broke through her hazed drowsiness.

Very clearly, with great dignity, she said, 'Randal, you are not to seduce me.'

His mouth laughed against her cheek. 'I'm not in the habit of seducing children,' he murmured teasingly.

'Then what are you doing?' she asked, feeling a tremor of delight as his lashes tickled against her skin in a soft butterfly kiss.

'What does one do to children?' he asked. 'I'm amusing you.'

The answer satisfied her. 'Oh,' she said trustingly, leaning back against his arm, aware vaguely of the muscled strength of the flesh beneath the sleeve.

He pressed a brief kiss on each of her closed lids. 'I am amusing you, aren't I?' he asked gently.

'I'm not sure what you're doing,' she yawned. 'But I like it.'

Her honesty made him silent, staring down into the small face with a grimness which took all the humour out of his mouth. He wanted badly to kiss her into awareness of him, but she was as confiding as a baby against him, and his mouth twisted sardonically.

His immobility percolated to her. Her lids lifted. She gazed at him, seeing, at close quarters, the hard bone structure of his face, the self-controlled blue eyes, the stubborn jawline and, with a new realisation, a certain sensual promise implicit in the line of his mouth.

Dreamily she lifted a hand and ran a finger along

his lips. 'I have a feeling you aren't to be trusted, Mr Randal Saxton,' she said directly. 'Not with that mouth.'

The humour came back to his face. 'My God,' he said, half breathlessly, 'I'm not as dangerous as you are, Marcy. Have you any idea what you're doing to me?'

She looked uneasy. 'I think I'd better go,' she said, shifting to escape him.

He retrieved her without difficulty, his arms tightening around her with an instinctive, unmistakable movement of possession. 'I want you, Marcy,' he said suddenly, his voice sober.

She was as still as a wary animal, staring at his face. The tone in which he had said it did not frighten her, but his suddenly grave face did.

Still suffering from the after-effect of the wine, she said clearly, 'Would you care to expand on that remark?'

His gravity vanished in a mocking little smile. 'Now who's being pompous?'

'You can't just say things like that to me without making it clear what you mean,' she frowned, struggling to make herself clear.

'I could make myself overwhelmingly clear without any trouble at all,' Randal said wryly. But you're slightly tipsy, Marcy, and that would be unfair tactics.'

'Ah, a sign of moral principles at last,' she said lucidly, her eyes teasing him.

His face altered again. There was abrupt passion in the blue eyes. 'You irritating, irresistible child,' he said thickly, and began to kiss her with a desire which blazed out of him unleashed and utterly shocked and stunned her.

No one had ever subjected her to such a demonstration of passion, and although she lay unresisting beneath his assault, she was taken aback and staggered by it. His hand slid under her wild mop of hair, shaping her nape with his warm palm, caressing and holding her beneath his hungry mouth. Marcy was brought abruptly out of her sleepy trance as unexpected, unexperienced quivers of feeling began to erupt all over her slender body. Without being able to think under the storm which was engulfing her, she began to kiss him back, her soft lips so novice as she did so that Randal was almost touched, except that the quivering movements she was making were sending wild sensations of delight through his whole body and making him spin rapidly beyond hope of regaining control.

Realising he had to put the brake on his own passion, he sharply pulled back his head, breathing fast. Marcy lay, with tightly closed eyes and parted mouth, a passionate, helpless sweetness in her face.

'I think,' said Randal carefully, 'that I'd better drive you home now.'

He stood her up, but she staggered, still under the influence of her own passionate abandonment. He caught her, his arms holding her close to his lean body, and she confidingly leaned her head against him. Randal stared down at her, his mouth wry. 'You're just a baby,' he said, half ruefully.

'I'm so sleepy,' she yawned. 'Oh, please, let me go to sleep.'

Randal bit his lower lip, frowning. Then he lifted her entirely into his arms and carried her out of the room.

Walters, hovering in the hall, with an undisguised anxiety in his face, watched in disbelief as his master silently carried her up the stairs.

Randal bore her into a large, charmingly furnished bedroom and laid her on the white and gold bed. Her lids remained shut. She breathed gently, her slight limbs relaxed. Randal made a face at his own folly, then slid her tenderly between the sheets, still fully dressed, tucked her in carefully, and went out, turning out the light.

He went downstairs again. Walters still hovered there, discreetly looking at him with a question in those pouched eyes.

'Bring me some brandy,' Randal said.

Walters vanished and returned to hand him a glass. Randal surveyed him drily. 'You can go to bed, Walters.'

Walters shifted from foot to foot. 'The young lady, sir,' he said unhappily.

'Is fast asleep like all good little girls,' Randal said with hard mockery.

Walters looked at him uneasily.

'Oh, go to bed,' muttered Randal. 'I've no designs on the child, for God's sake!'

'No, sir,' Walters murmured politely, reassured, and silently departed.

Randal tossed off the brandy, grimacing. He gazed

at the ceiling as if speaking to the girl fast asleep in bed exactly overhead. 'Marcy Campion, you incredible child, I must be out of my mind!' he told her aloud.

Marcy woke up with a distinct impression that something was tickling her nose. She snorted, pushing at it with one hand, but the tickling recommenced a moment later, and reluctantly she opened her eyes, staring incredulously at the face staring back at her.

Slowly, thinking quickly, she looked around the room in which she found herself. It was a bedroom which had been furnished with a woman in mind, she thought, taking in the delicacy of the white and gold furnishings, the muted shades of the floral carpet, the golden walls. Randal said nothing, did not move, observing her reactions with a wry interest.

She looked down at her dress, then up at him, in his dark office suit and blue and white striped shirt.

'That wine,' she said on a sigh.

His mouth grinned. 'You've no head, little Marcy.'

'You should have taken me home,' she pointed out reprovingly.

'And missed the chance of getting you into bed?' he asked mockingly.

She fluttered her gilt-tipped lashes at him. 'You may be what Russell calls a bloated capitalist, but you don't use methods like that,' she said lightly.

His fingers played with her tousled bright hair. 'You offered me a hell of a temptation,' he murmured.

Their eyes met. She felt a strange confusion right in the middle of her body. She looked away. 'Are you going to work now? You look very formal and top executive in that suit.'

'I've called a board meeting at eleven to discuss the Campion Project,' he said, leaning a hand across her slim body in the bed, so that he trapped her within a barrier of his arms.

'The what?' Bewilderment filled her face.

'Don't you remember? We discussed it last night.'

She gave a charmingly penitent smile. 'I don't remember much of anything we did last night,' she said casually.

His eyes flickered over her open, trusting face. 'Well, I'll draw up a typed schedule of what we outlined and you can refresh your memory,' he said, amused by what she had admitted. 'Basically, my plan was for the local people to decide exactly what the best use of the property should be . . .'

Marcy nodded soberly. 'That sounds reasonable. I'll get up and go back to talk it over with Sim.'

Randal tensed, watching her. 'Would it be possible for you to wait here for me for a few hours? I would like a chance to talk to the board first before any premature announcement is made.'

She fixed her green eyes on him. 'You think they may be difficult about it?'

'Saxtons stand to lose quite a lot of money over it,' he said.

She frowned. 'I thought you were the Great Panjandrum there?'

His mouth dented humorously. 'Even the general has to convince his army his plan of battle is sound,' he said.

She shrugged. 'When will you be back?'

'Have a long breakfast, then get Walters to find you something to read, or put on a record,' he said. 'I'll be back before lunchtime.'

'I can't just stay here . . .' she protested, frowning.

'Why not?'

The question threw her. She looked at him, her nose wrinkling. 'I only came to dinner,' she said plaintively. The green eyes were speculative. 'Randal, you frighten me.'

He smiled mockingly. 'Nothing frightens the girl from Paradise Street, surely?'

'You have a way of taking over things which is pretty alarming,' she observed. 'One minute I was at war with Saxtons, the next I find a take-over bid going on over my head without even realising it.'

'I think on my feet,' he said coolly.

'Just what do you think, though?' she mused, half to herself.

He touched her nose with one finger indulgently. 'I'll tell you when I have more time. Right now, I've got to go to that board meeting.'

She still looked at him apprehensively, and he sighed. 'Marcy, answer one question . . .'

'Yes?'

'Do you trust me?'

She felt the total gravity of the question and answered it in the same tone. 'Yes.'

He smiled with sudden charm. 'Then wait here patiently until I get back.'

When he had gone she lay staring at the closed door. She trusted him, and yet . . . there was this enormous question mark in her mind, and the trouble was she did not even know what the question was . . .

There was a knock at the door as she lay puzzling over her own thoughts. 'Come in,' she called cheerfully. Walters appeared, a faint smile on his pouched face, as carefully attired as he had been the previous evening.

'Good morning, miss,' he greeted her, carrying a cup of tea to her bedside. 'Mr Randal wondered if you would care to borrow some of Miss Anthea's clothes, seeing that you may wish to change before coming downstairs?'

'Who is Miss Anthea?' Marcy asked curiously.

'Mr Randal's sister, miss,' Walters explained. 'She is in Switzerland at school at present, but many of her clothes are in her room, and I think they will be the right size. Miss Anthea is more or less your build, miss.'

'That's very kind of Mr Randal,' said Marcy, grinning. What will Miss Anthea say, though?'

Walters looked confidentially at her. 'She is a very pleasant young lady. She would have no objections at all. Her room is just across the landing, miss—the first door opposite. Next to that is the bathroom. When you are ready, your breakfast will be served in the dining-room.'

'Thank you,' she said, watching him depart with his silent tread, her face reflecting her amusement. Randal Saxton thought of everything. His mind was, apparently, capable of small commonsense solutions to everyday problems as well as the task of juggling with the difficulties of high finance.

When she had drunk her tea she went across the landing and peeped in at a delightfully furnished room, all roseate and feminine, which yet betrayed its owner as an adolescent by the large wall posters displayed along one side—enormous photographs of masculine stars of the pop world and films.

She opened the wall wardrobe which occupied the whole of one side of the room. The door slid back softly to reveal row upon row of clothes which made her gasp. How on earth could one girl ever wear so many? She flicked them through her fingers, admiring them, then stood, grimacing for a moment. In any of them she would feel unreal, as different from her own personality as she had felt last night, seated in that dining-room beside Randal.

With hesitation she took down a black velvet trouser suit which caught her eye, and held it out at arms' length to stare at it with pleasure. She had never worn anything like it in her life, but she wanted badly to wear it now. She looked down at her own green dress, crumpled where she had slept in it last night, and a blaze of sudden defiance lit her eyes. Why shouldn't she?

Fifteen minutes later, having showered and spent some time dressing, she stared at herself in the mirror with incredulity. The reflection which stared back at her was almost a stranger.

Without giving herself time to argue, she went downstairs and found Walters hovering in the hall. He gave her a quick, surprised look, and she grinned at him.

'Clothes make the man, don't they?'

'You look very charming, miss,' said Walters, ushering her into the dining-room. 'Your breakfast will be ready immediately, miss.'

She looked around the elaborate formality of the room with a grimace. 'Do I have to eat it in here?'

He looked taken aback. 'Well, miss . . .'

'Couldn't I eat in the kitchen?'

Walters looked as aghast as if she had suggested something disgraceful. 'Anatole, miss,' he began.

'The French chef,' she said, her eyes amused. 'I'm dying to meet him. A mythical French chef in captivity . . . as rare as a dodo.'

'They are extinct, miss,' Walters informed her with a trace of humour.

Marcy walked out of the dining-room. 'Which is the way to the kitchen?' she asked, then, by instinct, turned through the green baize door she saw and Walters, muttering under his breath, followed her.

The kitchen occupied the basement, she found, running down a flight of stairs. When she halted in the long, bright room she found herself face to face with a very thin, melancholy man in a striped apron who was whisking something in a metal basin, his wrist flicking effortlessly at great speed.

Walters stood behind her, staring in consternation at the other man, whose gloomy expression darkened as he met her inquisitive eyes.

Marcy smiled, her green eyes full of friendliness. 'Hallo, you must be the marvellous Anatole I've been hearing about. I'm Marcy.' She sniffed. 'What a wonderful smell. What's cooking?'

Anatole's spaniel eyes seemed to rivet on her face

as she prowled around the room, admiring the highly efficient, modern kitchen.

'Miss wondered if she could eat her breakfast down here,' Walters told him uneasily.

'I'm starving,' Marcy informed Anatole, turning to smile at him, her whole face filled with that childlike radiance which was her most obvious attraction. 'I know I shouldn't be after the pig I made of myself last night. The dinner was the best I've ever eaten in my life. I don't know how you can bear to cook for one man when you could be running some enormous hotel kitchen. You're wasted here.'

Anatole stood the metal basin on the table, and put his hands on his hips, staring at her. 'I cook for Mr Saxton because he pays me very well,' he said in perfect English.

She blinked. 'I thought you were French.'

'I am,' he said, sniffing. 'If you wish, I can speak in pidgin English . . . for Mr Saxton's guests I do so. They like it.'

She laughed. 'Well, plain English will do for me. I'm not a guest.'

The two men looked at each other over her marigold head. Anatole moved to the hotplate and began to make her breakfast. Walters stood with a dubious countenance, as if wondering what to do next. Marcy looked round at him.

'Come and talk to me, Mr Walters,' she invited.

Anatole looked round at him sardonically.

Walters slowly drew back a chair and sat down. Marcy grinned at him. 'How long have you worked for Mr Saxton?'

'I worked for his father, miss,' Walters said. 'I came to this house when I was twenty years old.'

'Tell me about his father,' Marcy invited, smiling acceptance as Anatole placed fresh orange juice in front of her.

'Well, I . . .' Walters looked uncomfortable.

'Did he look like Randal?' Marcy asked, sipping pleasurably as the ice-cold tingle of the fruit juice trickled down her throat.

'Very similar, miss,' Walters admitted. 'He was a very remote man—clever, hard-headed, but remote. Business was his whole life.'

'And Randal's mother?'

Walters smiled. 'A charming lady. She was delicate, though, I'm afraid. Miss Anthea's birth took a toll on her health. She died when Mr Randal was in his last year at school. It hit him very hard.'

'How old is Miss Anthea?'

'Seventeen, miss.'

'Not much younger than me,' smiled Marcy.

Anatole, placing a silver dish on the table, glanced at Walters with a saturnine expression. Marcy missed the glance the two men exchanged as she took egg, bacon and kidney from the dish and hungrily began to eat.

She drank several cups of extremely good coffee, then sat talking to Walters as Anatole prepared the lunch, her laughter ringing out as Walters quietly told her some anecdotes about Anthea Saxton, who, it seemed, was very fond of practical jokes, especially ones which punctured her brothers sense of self-importance.

'If you had a pack of cards I could tell your fortune,' she informed Anatole with a wicked smile. 'There were some gypsies who came to our district every summer, and one of the women taught me to tell fortunes.'

'I do not believe in fortune telling,' Anatole said loftily.

'Neither do I, silly,' Marcy retorted. 'But it's fun.'

Walters went to a cupboard and produced a pack of cards, giving Anatole a defiant glare. The three of them sat down around the table, and Marcy began to shuffle the cards.

Returning from his board meeting with a wry smile on his face after a long, incredulous struggle with his fellow directors, Randal let himself into his house, feeling a leap of the heart as he walked into the sitting-room in search of Marcy. Finding no sign of her, he frowned, his blue eyes darkening in disappointment. Had she, after all, gone back to Paradise Street without waiting for him? A sensation of sharp anger made his brows black above the calm mask of his usual expression. He walked to the baize door to open it, intending to shout for Walters, sheer impotent frustration making him too annoyed to ring.

From below came the soft peal of laughter. His rage vanished and a flicker of surprised amusement came into his face. Softly he crept down the stairs. He rarely ventured into the kitchen domain ruled over by Anatole and it was a long time since he had been down there. At the back of the room he stood watching the three heads close together around the table. Anatole was laughing, his normally melancholy glumness banished, his dark eyes snapping. Walters was making soft, smothered sounds closely resembling chuckles.

'It's all true,' Marcy protested demurely. 'See, it says so in the cards . . .'

'So,' said Anatole, his usually perfect English deserting him, 'and when my racehorse has won the Derby? Shall I be even richer?'

'Fabulously,' Marcy said solemnly. 'You'll make a take-over bid for Saxtons and you'll generously employ Mr Randal as your chef.'

Anatole's laughter redoubled. He moved backwards, his face writhing with it, and his dark eyes fell upon Randal's cool, satirical face. Horror flashed into Anatole's features and he almost fell over as he jumped up. Walters turned, gasped and went a pale shade of green. Marcy looked over her shoulder and grinned unrepentantly at the new arrival.

'Come and have your fortune told, Randal,' she offered him sweetly.

The two servants grew suddenly busy, each vanishing in opposite directions. Randal strolled over to the table and looked down at the cards. 'Later, perhaps,' he said lightly. 'Just now I think we'll let Anatole get on with the lunch.'

Marcy shrugged. 'It's ready,' she said. 'We're going to have . . .'

'Never mind that,' said Randal, his hand lifting her slight body upward. 'Come along, child. Stop getting in Anatole's way.'

She allowed him to usher her back upstairs into the hall. There she gave him a rueful smile. 'I don't think I annoyed Anatole, really.'

'I suspect you enchanted him,' Randal observed blandly. 'Especially with your final prediction.'

She laughed. 'Are you afraid I may have undermined feudal discipline, Randal?'

'I should have known better than to leave dynamite lying around unattended in this house,' he said drily, but his blue eyes were moving over her in a strangely concentrated fashion, making her curiously aware of him.

Marcy felt a heat in her cheeks. To cover it, she twirled around in front of him, her arms lifted. 'What do you think? I hope your sister won't be offended by my borrowing her clothes. I'll have them cleaned for her before I return them.'

'You look like a boy,' he said softly. 'Just until one looks closer and sees more clearly . . .'

He was certainly looking closer, she thought in a flicker of rebellion, feeling his roving eyes intensely. He took her hand lightly and pulled her into the sitting-room, pushing her down on to the couch. 'Have some sherry?'

He was already pouring the amber liquid behind her as she turned her head to refuse, so she took the glass he offered and sipped at it.

He sat down beside her and turned to look at her, his smooth features unrevealing as he surveyed the frilled white lace of her blouse, the tight-fitting black velvet jacket with its open lapels, the slightly flared black velvet pants. Above, her astonishing hair blazed around her face, the fine curls making his fingers itch to touch them.

'Tell me about the board meeting,' she invited.

He shrugged. 'No doubt you can remember days in Cornwall when the winds raged, the seas crashed back and forwards and it wasn't safe to put one's head out of doors.'

'As bad as that?' she asked, sympathetically.

'I understate the situation,' he assured her wryly.

'Poor Randal!'

He gave her a narrow-eyed look. 'You don't ask who won?'

She put her sherry glass down and put her linked arms above her head, stretching lazily. 'I'm beginning to know you too well.'

He put his own glass down, watching the slender boyish length of her extended body out of his side-ways glance. 'I'm touched by your confidence.'

'So this afternoon we can tell Sim?' she asked.

He swivelled, frowning. 'If you like,' he said slowly, eyeing her. 'Aren't you warm in that jacket indoors? Take it off.'

Marcy sat forward. 'It looks so nice,' she said childishly, 'I prefer to keep it on.'

His smile was indulgent. 'It may look nicer, but your face is flushed,' he said, firmly beginning to remove it.

She struggled, a queer panic in her throat. He paused, staring at her. 'Stop running my life, Randal,' she said huskily. 'You make me feel . . .'

'What do I make you feel?' he asked as her voice broke off.

'Threatened,' she said in a low tone.

He slid a cool hand under her chin, lifting her face. 'Threatened in what way?'

'How do I know?' she returned. 'You're too managing, too bossy.'

A flicker of thought passed over his face. Just as if, she thought, he were disappointed by her answer.

'Keep your jacket on if you must,' he said, releasing her with an abrupt gesture.

She slid out of it. 'No, you're right. It is too warm.'

His mouth twisted sardonically. 'You contrary child.'

'Stop calling me a child!'

His face moved closer, his eyes riveted on her face. 'Do you resent it?'

'You treat me as if I were your little sister!'

'Do I, by God?' he retorted with a snort of laughter, and her spine suddenly prickled uneasily at something in his tone. She moved discreetly away, watching him cautiously. 'Tell me what really happened at the board meeting,' she invited.

He slid an arm along the couch, leaning over her, his eyes fixed on her pink mouth. 'Changing the subject, Marcy?' he asked teasingly. 'You issued a challenge just now and you know it . . .' His other hand moved slowly along her arm. She felt the warmth of his palm through the fine lace, and was conscious of a feeling of acute tension, a sensation so new to her that she was taken aback by it.

Nervously, she asked, 'How long do you think it will take before we can see the new plans for the development?'

Randal's arousing hand had reached her thin shoulder. 'I've already set the wheels in motion,' he told her, staring at the fine shoulder bones his fingers were slowly exploring. 'You're so tiny I feel I could break you with one hand, Marcy,' he said softly.

There was something insidiously pleasant about his hands touching her. It made her feel acutely nervous. 'I . . . I wonder how long Anatole will be serving lunch,' she said, turning to glance at the door.

'You weren't as nervous as this last night,' Randal observed indolently.

Her gaze flashed to his face, wide and startled. 'What?'

His hard mouth was lazily mocking as he saw the look on her small features. 'In fact, I would have called you very co-operative.'

Her green eyes searched his blue ones intently. 'Oh,' she said, flushing. 'The wine . . .'

His hand was winding itself into her wild bright hair. 'Yes,' he agreed blandly. 'The wine, little Marcy.' And then he moved, and she closed her eyes, experiencing the full sensation of what he was doing to her, totally alert this morning, as she had not been the night before, feeling the gentle, searching sensuality of his kiss in every nerve of her body. Randal made no violent or alarming demands upon her. His hard mouth explored her parted lips, gently caressing them, and she found the sensation so pleasant that her slight body swayed quite involuntarily towards him, and his hands at once pulled her closer.

She could feel one move up along her back, pushing into her fine hair, stroking her nape with sensitive fingers, letting the marmalade-coloured curls entwine around his hand. The effect of what he was doing was very odd, she thought dreamily. Tentatively, half alarmed, she slid her hands up his shirt to his neck, and he made a sound against the soft mouth he was caressing, an odd, muffled sound which surprised her.

As if her own movement had brought about an alteration in him, the cautious gentleness of the kiss became different. He tilted her head, his hands holding it between their palms, and she felt urgency in the demanding pressure on her mouth.

Dazed and utterly new to the feelings which she could feel surging through him, she trembled, moved by an inexplicable desire to give him the response he was asking for, kissing him back, her warm mouth tender. Randal began to breathe as if he were fighting for life. His hands left her hair and began to move down her back, shaping her between them in a curiously exciting, alarming fashion. One hand moved over her midriff. Suddenly she felt it close over her small breast, and Randal's heartbeat grew louder. Marcy, shocked out of her trance, pulled violently away from him.

'No,' she said shakily, putting her hands up to push him away.

He was very flushed. The blue eyes seemed to flicker with fire. For a moment they looked at each other, then, restlessly, he moved away. 'I'm sorry,' he said after a pause, his voice shaky. 'I lost my head.'

She looked down, smoothing the black velvet with nervous fingers. 'Randal, I'm only just eighteen. I know that these days girls of my age are often very used to kissing and boy-friends, but I've been brought up rather differently, and I feel far too young to get involved with someone like you . . .'

'What about Sim?' he asked her, his body rigid, yet filled with that nervous, restless energy.

She turned scarlet. 'Sim?' Dismay filled her eyes.

His face hardened. He watched her with sudden remorseless closeness. 'I saw him kiss you yesterday,' he reminded her. 'I would say he could give me a few years.'

'That's different,' she said uneasily.

'Why is it?' he asked harshly. 'Are you in love with him?'

She looked down, embarrassment in her face. 'Randal, I really don't want to talk about it to you. Please, can't you ring for lunch? I'm sure poor Anatole has been waiting downstairs for ages with his marvellous food getting cold.'

Randal looked as if he wanted to say something explosive, but after a grim pause he furiously rang for Walters to serve the lunch.

CHAPTER FOUR

THEY drove back to Paradise Street in the middle of the warm summer afternoon, through London roads jammed with traffic, children eating icecream, perspiring policemen in the crisp dark blue of shirt sleeve order which in England always indicates a swing to hot weather, girls in summer dresses sauntering casually where in winter they would be hurrying with bent heads, and the sudden appearance of icecream vans, soft drink stalls and workmen digging roads in bare brown-chested cheerfulness. The whole atmosphere of the sprawling city had swung into the summer atmosphere of casual enjoyment of life.

Randal parked beside the house and the two of them wandered across the garden. A few invisible inhabitants tensed, peering through the pale summer-bleached stalks of grass, bright eyes glinting. Marcy shouted, 'Why aren't you at school? If you get caught it serves you right!' and opened the front door. Randal looked around, having missed the few slight signs which betrayed other presences to her. Then followed her into the grubby, shabby hall.

'Children?' he asked.

She grinned. 'A few of them bunk out when they feel like it . . . they'd bunk out anyway, but having Paradise Street to come to, they make for here now.'

'Bunk out?' Randal's fine brows lifted.

'Skip school . . . play truant.' She gave him her confidential, teasing smile. 'I'll have to give you a vocabulary lesson before I let you loose on the local inhabitants. You're in foreign territory here, Randal.'

'I'm beginning to realise it,' he agreed. His eyes wandered through the hall, narrowing. 'This could be a very fine property,' he murmured. 'It's been allowed to run down appallingly, but the shell of it is still worth preserving. Did you say the local preservation group were interested?'

'Sim roped them in,' she nodded.

His glance at her was unrevealing. 'Could you get hold of Sim? Ask him to come over and look around the house with me?'

'I'll ring him, shall I?' She moved to the door. 'Why don't you look around the house while I'm ringing his office? I'm not sure he'll be there—sometimes he has to go to court or to visit one of his clients in prison.'

She left him walking around the lower rooms and ran to the nearest callbox. It was vandalised beyond repair, so, grimacing, she ran into the betting shop in Crancy Alley, and asked Mr Wills, the owner, if she could use his telephone. His yellow teeth glinting at her, Mr Wills waved a friendly hand. 'Help yourself, darling.' His grandson, Micky, was one of her regular visitors, a boy of eight with a shrewd quick mind who had a natural talent for mathematics and hated school.

When she had rung Sim's office, and found him absent but expected back any moment, she left a message for him to come to Paradise Street and left the shop, smiling goodbye to the men studying form with more passion than they had ever shown their wives.

Before returning to the house she paused to offer a bag of jelly beans to the still invisible inhabitants of the garden, laying it on the path with a shouted, 'Fair shares and no fighting!'

Hearing Randal's footsteps on the bare boards upstairs, she stood in the hall, shouting, 'I'll make some tea. Want some?'

'Thank you,' he called back. 'I'll be down in a moment. Some of this stuff is incredible!'

Marcy went into the dark, spider-haunted kitchen and began to make tea. She put out two cups and some shortcake biscuits, then, hearing someone bang on the front door, went to answer it, her slight figure graceful in the black velvet suit, expecting Sim.

She opened it with a welcoming smile, but her expression changed as she saw Lisa in the doorway. The older woman's face was charged with hostility. Marcy's green eyes flickered.

'Oh, hello,' she said, a little breathlessly.

Lisa came into the hall and slammed the door shut. Marcy fell back a pace or two, sensing that Lisa was in a very angry mood. They faced each other in silence for a moment. Lisa's cold eyes moved over the black velvet suit, the lace shirt, the obviously expensive look of the whole outfit. Her mouth took on an acid smile.

'So,' she said nastily, 'the little girl from Paradise Street wears something better than old jeans and T-shirts now, does she? I wonder who paid for that?

I suppose it wouldn't have come from my Sim, by any chance ?'

Marcy's whole body seemed to be covered in heated embarrassment. 'No,' she said indignantly. 'Lisa . . .'

'Don't you Lisa me,' the other snorted. 'Mrs Gold to you.' She emphasised the name savagely. 'I suppose it should have occurred to me a long time ago, but Sim's always getting involved in some cranky cause or other, and this time seemed no different. When he brought me here I only had to look at you to dismiss you from my mind . . . a scruffy little kid in jeans . . . who'd have thought my Sim would be weak-minded enough to look twice at you?' Her smooth, petal-soft skin convulsed in a bitter rage. As carefully, expertly made up as ever, in her expensive, well-cut dress, the veneer of cool hauteur had been stripped away overnight and Lisa's acquisitive, possessive feelings for Sim shone through.

'Lisa, you're wrong,' Marcy said desperately. 'Sim loves you.'

'Yes,' Lisa hissed. 'And what's more, he's mine. I'm his wife, little Miss Paradise Street, and I understand him better than you ever could. I've known Sim most of my life. My family knows his family. If you think I'll give him up without a fight you're way off course, let me tell you . . . I know the way to keep Sim, and I'll keep him.' A flash of envious, bitter emotion crossed her beautiful face. 'Just because you're a young girl, that's all it is. He feels he's getting older and he wants to prove he can still attract young women. It's just a phase. Once he's got a child of his own he won't get wandering eyes again. I'll see to that.'

'I know Sim wants a child,' said Marcy, half stunned by the torrent of angry words.

'From me!' Lisa half screamed. 'From me, not you. Oh, he's been looking at you, he admitted as much, but last night he came back to me, Miss Marcy Campion, and I'm going to see he has nothing more to do with you and your mad schemes. I'll tell the press what sort of girl you are, chasing married men . . . I'll call them and give them the truth about you!'

Marcy was struck dumb with horror, staring at her. Behind them there was a knock at the door. Automatically she groped for the handle and opened it. Russell and a little band of reporters and photographers stood on the doorstep, excitement oozing out of them as they poured across the threshold. Marcy looked, aghast, at Lisa, her green eyes imploring her. Had Lisa rung them to invite them here to be told her sordid little story?

Before either of the two of them had recovered from the surprise of the invasion, Randal Saxton slowly came down the stairs, his blue eyes fixed on Marcy's white, stunned face.

Some wild instinct took her to his side, her eyes raised to his face, silently begging him to help her. He slid an arm around the slender figure, pulling her possessively against his lean, strong body, and, with a yielding sigh, she turned her face into the material of his dark suit, leaving the situation entirely to him.

The reporters began firing questions at him. 'Is it true, Mr Saxton, that your firm have suddenly reversed their policy about the development? Why have you changed your minds? What do you now intend to do?' Their voices shouted one above the other, the questions interrupting each other in a babbled din.

Photographers scrambled to take pictures of Randal Saxton, his arm in unmistakable protection, around Marcy's slight figure.

Randal held up his long hand, a look of calm authority on his hard face. 'Please, gentlemen. I shall make one statement, and that must suffice for all of you. All future press releases on the subject will be made by my press office.'

The babble broke out again, but he quelled it with a crisp, icy voice. 'Shut up! Now, Miss Marcy Campion and myself are engaged to be married.' In the firm circle of his arms a protesting, incredulous movement from the slight figure was quelled ruthlessly, his hand on her bright curls, forcing her head into his jacket. 'In consequence, the difficulties about the development are now over. This house and the garden will be made into an integral part of the development, to be called in the future, The Campion Centre. My fiancée wishes the people of the borough themselves to decide what to do with the centre. There will be full democratic involvement at public meetings. A committee will be formed of local people to draw up plans. My firm will place an architect at their disposal to assist them.' He gave them all a polite, formal smile. 'That's all, gentlemen. Good day.'

If Randal had seriously imagined that he would get away with making such a statement without being

bombarded with questions, he was wrong. The air
was thick with shouted words. Reporters jostled to
bellow at him. Marcy, held against him protectively,
heard their voices in a muffled bellow, like angry
bulls, and pressed closer, shivering, so that his hand
comfortingly stroked her hair, his thumb finding her
slender nape and rubbing it soothingly, sensing the
alarm and tension inside her.

Lisa Gold stood to one side, staring out of dis-
believing yet astounded eyes at the two of them.
Randal was at bay, protecting Marcy, the whole attitude of the way he held her telling its own story.

'Can we have a picture of you and Miss Campion,
sir?' a small, sharp-faced photographer asked, his
hand plucking at Marcy's slender arm.

Randal's free hand moved to push him away, a
sudden rage in his face. 'Leave her alone!'

Lisa, swept aside in the stampede, saw the look in
the handsome, hard face, and her woman's instinct
told her that however Sim might have felt about
Marcy, this man was the man in possession. Every
look he threw down at the small body in his arms said
as much. Her slim shoulders lowered in a sigh. She
had made a fool of herself, and she was irritated by
the thought.

'Just one picture,' the photographers pleaded.
'We've taken pictures of Miss Campion before, sir.
Our readers will want to see the two of you kiss-
ing . . .'

Marcy quivered. Randal looked down at the wild,
marmalade mop of her hair, thinking fast. He was
afraid to release her in case she denied their engage-

ment. He inwardly cursed the photographers, then his strong hands held her away from him and in a deft, swift movement, his mouth came down to close over hers before she could speak.

Her green eyes glared at him helplessly, then a gasp came from the small mouth as the violence and passion in his kiss reached her, and involuntarily the small white lids closed, the lashes fluttering down against her flushed cheek. Her arms slid round his neck, her whole slight body curved towards him. Flashbulbs exploded all around them. Marcy felt them like fireworks under her closed lids. All she could think of was the extraordinary sweetness of what Randal was doing to her.

Sim, arriving at that moment, having received Marcy's message, stared incredulously over the thronged heads of the journalists, seeing Randal Saxton with his arms tightly laced around the body of the slight girl in her black velvet suit, the lightning of flashbulbs illuminating them, as they kissed with a passion which was clear to everyone who looked at them.

Lisa, catching sight of him, slid around the back of the crowd, to touch his arm. Sim looked at her in surprise, flushing. Last night Lisa had been vitriolic, far too quick to guess exactly who he had been tempted to look at more than once, and he wondered what exactly she was doing here. Her smile took him aback.

'Fancy that little kid catching a man like Randal Saxton,' she said, a slight envy in her tone mingling with the relief she was feeling. Marcy's embarrassed reaction to her tirade now made her feel stupid. She had been wrong in her accusations. Whatever had been in her Sim's mind had not been in the mind of the girl. Much as Lisa loved her Sim, she was not fool enough to imagine anyone turning down a millionaire for an East End solicitor.

'What's going on?' Sim asked huskily.

'They're engaged,' said Lisa, looking at him in sudden compassion. It occurred to her that beneath his interest in that girl must be a deep longing for a daughter of his own, a child to whom he could show all his tenderness. She touched his cheek, her eyes approving his distinguished appearance. He was worth looking at, her Sim. He looked at her and she smiled at him.

'You know, if I don't have a baby soon I'll be too old to enjoy it,' she said.

Sim's breath seemed to stop. Delight broke out on his face. 'Oh, Lisa,' he said shakily. Behind them the hubbub continued, and he looked round at the press irritably. 'I'd better put a stop to this,' he said. He pushed his way through the crowd and caught his brother's arm. 'Get them out, Russ.'

'Have a heart,' said Russell. 'This is the story of the year. What a twist! Let the dog see the rabbit.'

'Can we have a statement from the girl? She hasn't said a word yet,' a journalist called.

'Can we have a smile, Mr Saxton?' a photographer shouted.

'Hold hands, Marcy,' another hissed.

'Get out of the way!' a photographer snarled at Sim, elbowing him.

Randal had released Marcy's mouth with reluctance, but he was staring down at her tenderly, and she was gazing at him, a strange, distraught, incredulous flickering smile on her mouth. The way he had kissed her had totally astonished her, and his announcement seemed almost to have been pushed to the back of her mind by the shock of his passion.

Randal looked round and saw Sim. Naked antagonism came into Randal's face, and the two men stared at each other. The reporters shouted questions. Randal asked Marcy, 'Do you feel up to talking to the bastards?'

'What shall I say?' she asked submissively.

'Just take my lead,' he said.

Questions flew like missiles from all directions. Randal answered them when he could, and Marcy softly made parrying replies when forced to do so. She held Randal's hand, they smiled at each other, flashbulbs dazzled her.

'Where's the ring?' one asked.

'Being altered,' said Randal blandly. 'Too big for her hand,' and he lifted one of them to demonstrate the fine small fingers, bending his dark head to kiss it gracefully. The photographers palpitated, snatching pictures of the movement.

'What's the ring like?' a reporter asked.

Randal glanced into Marcy's incredulous, anxious eyes. 'An emerald,' he said coolly. 'A family ring.'

A woman reporter pushed a fascinated head through the ring of faces. 'Is it a family heirloom, Mr Saxton?'

Randal nodded.

'How long have you known Marcy? When's the wedding? When did you propose?' Questions flooded at them and left Marcy blinking, dazed.

'I fell in love with her at first sight,' Randal explained in his bland, polite voice. 'We're getting married as soon as possible.'

The clamour of voices seemed to swell. Marcy was feeling cold and weak. A buzzing in her head sounded as if a flock of bees had flown in through her ears. She looked at Randal imploringly, giving a muffled cry, and his head swung to her in alarm just as she slid to the floor. Sim moved anxiously, but Randal had already gathered her up into his arms, her bright head falling back over his sleeve while his hard face looked at her in white anxiety. The photographers almost died of excitement, snapping like sharks around them, filling the dark hall with the brilliance of flashbulbs.

'My God, you vultures, leave her alone!' Randal snarled, pushing past them. 'You,' he said savagely to Sim. 'Get them all out of here.'

Sim shepherded the journalists and photographers towards the door, Russell reluctantly aiding him, rounding up obstinate strays who tried to dart into the room where Randal had carried Marcy, pushing them all out of the front door with threats about the police, until at last they were all gone, and the house seemed almost eerily silent.

Russell leaned against the door, grinning, a low soft whistle on his mouth. 'That little kid . . . who'd have thought it? She's pulled one surprise after

another . . . her and Randal Saxton. Sim, did she
give you any clue?'

'Hadn't you better phone your story through?'
Sim asked him flatly.

'God,' Russell groaned, running a hand through
his hair, 'I must be losing my mind!' He pulled open
the door and vanished.

Sim stood, his hands in his pockets, staring at the
floor. Lisa glided to him with her swaying model's
walk and slid her hand through his arm. He turned to
look at her and gave her a smile.

'Well, quite a shock for everyone,' he commented.
'So Paradise Street is here to stay . . . it will mean a
lot of work. I know these committees. Talk, talk, talk
before anything gets done.'

'I've got to get to work,' said Lisa. Her eyes
caressed his face. 'I'll see you tonight, darling.'

Sim kissed her tenderly. 'You can take a bet on
that,' he grinned.

Lisa swayed out of the door and Sim turned to look
at the closed door behind which Marcy was with
Randal Saxton. He remembered her words about 'a
date' who would surprise him. Well, it had surprised
everyone. Yet he was not surprised. She was capable
of anything, that little girl.

Behind the closed door Randal was kneeling beside
Marcy's prone figure, watching as her eyelids stirred
reluctantly. She opened them and looked round at
him. Her face was still so white it made him sick with
anxiety and she looked unbelievably fragile, as
though one touch might shatter her into a million
fragments.

She sighed. 'Have they all gone?'

'All gone,' he agreed.

'I made some tea before they arrived, but it must be stone cold by now,' she said.

'I'll make some more.'

Her hand caught at his sleeve. 'No. Wait, Randal.'

He looked down, his face becoming wary. 'Yes?'

'Why did you do it?' she asked him breathlessly. 'Why on earth did you say that?'

'You were in a spot,' he said. 'You were asking me for help.'

Her lashes flickered with embarrassment. She remembered the alarm with which she had gone to him as he came down the stairs, begging him silently to do something. Lisa's threat had unnerved her for a moment.

'You shouldn't have told them such huge lies,' she said, faint colour returning to her face. 'I mean, sooner or later it will have to be proved to be a lie. We aren't engaged, Randal.'

His smile was bland. 'Of course we are.'

She gasped. 'You know we aren't!'

'I stated it publicly, my darling, and you didn't deny it,' he said mockingly. 'That constitutes a formal declaration of intent, wouldn't you say?'

Marcy sat upright abruptly. 'Randal, what are you up to?' she demanded. 'What do you think you're doing?'

He sat down beside her on the broken old sofa and grinned annoyingly at her. 'I'm turning a disastrous defeat into a victory of magnificent proportions,' he murmured.

Her quick green eyes surveyed him. 'Are you talking about Saxtons or about us?'

A strange cold hardness came into his face. 'Both,' he said. 'Are you going to tell me about Sim, Marcy?'

She was instantly scarlet. 'You heard!'

'His wife made no effort to keep her voice down,' he said drily. 'What fire was there beneath the smoke, Marcy?' He searched her green eyes intently. 'I saw him with you once, remember. He kissed you. So don't tell me there was nothing.'

She looked down, plaiting her thin small fingers into a web. 'It was nothing. Nothing to speak of . . .'

'A kiss? Or more than one kiss, I'd say,' said Randal harshly. 'From a married man of his age to a child of yours?'

Marcy made a quivering movement of the shoulders, a sigh. 'He was unhappy . . . he—liked me. All he did was look, Randal, and that stopped after I'd spoken to him.'

'All he did was look,' Randal repeated grimly. His hand raised her lowered head, forced her to look at him. 'He wanted you.'

'Not like that,' she protested, ashamed and angry. 'You make it sound . . . horrible! Sim's kind and sweet . . .'

'I'm sure he is,' said Randal sourly. 'I'm sure he wanted to be as kind and sweet as you would let him be. I've seen the way he looks at you . . .' And he recognised it, he thought with sickening jealousy.

'Sim loves his wife,' said Marcy. 'It was just an aberration.' The word came as a momentary inspira-

tion. 'He was miserable and he saw a lot of me, and
. . . and I like children . . .'

Randal bent a puzzled look on her face. 'What?'

'His wife wouldn't have any, and Sim's desperate,'
Marcy explained. 'That was really what it was all
about. He would never have fancied me otherwise.'

Randal's mouth softened into satire. 'So he fancied
you, did he? And did you fancy him, Marcy?'

'No!' She looked angry, then a flash of amusement
came into the green eyes and she gave him a curiously
provocative little smile, her lashes lowering. 'Well,
only the way most girls fancy good-looking older men
like you and Sim . . .'

Randal's face froze. He stared at the heart-shaped,
flushed face with eyes of blue ice. 'My God, you certainly hit below the belt, Marcy,' he said thickly.

She was puzzled, looking at him in surprise.
'What's wrong? I was teasing.'

'Teasing!' He said the word with angry emphasis,
and rose and moved away, his body taut with fierce
emotion. He stood with his back to her for a while,
his head averted, while she looked at him in bemused
wonder.

At last he turned and looked at her, his face cool.
'You can't stay here after this,' he said.

'Why not?' Her eyes widened.

'Have you any idea what sort of whirlwind is going
to be blowing around your unprotected head now
that this story has broken?' he asked wryly. 'The fuss
about the Paradise Street project is nothing compared
with the interest there's going to be in our engagement.'

'We'll just tell them we changed our minds,' she offered lightly, smiling at him.

'We haven't done anything of the kind,' Randal told her crisply.

'Randal!'

'I'm holding you to it,' he said, ignoring her cry of protest.

Marcy sat staring at him, her eyes growing very large. 'Randal, are you putting me in your pocket?' she asked after a moment.

The question made him laugh involuntarily. A wry smile made his blue eyes gleam. 'That's about the size of it,' he agreed blandly.

She looked indignant. 'You can't do that sort of thing to people,' she cried reprovingly. 'That may be how you go about acquiring firms and property, but not people, Randal!'

He came back, staring at her with blue eyes which danced and were insolently assured. 'But I'm doing it,' he said. 'I told you when you came to my house that I wanted you, Marcy. When I was a little boy I had a favourite book. It had the most marvellous illustrations in it. One of them was of a princess sitting beside a pond. She had golden curls just the same colour as yours, and great big eyes . . . I've still got the book safely locked away at home. And now I'm going to have you, too.'

Her face sobered incredulously. 'That's frightenng . . .' she murmured. 'Randal, you make me feel frightened.'

He sat down beside her again, turning her small head towards him with a warm, possessive hand, smiling into her alarmed green eyes. 'There's no need to be, Marcy. I look after what I own.'

'I don't want you to own me,' she said breathlessly. 'I'm a human being with feelings and a mind of my own. You wouldn't leave me room to breathe—you'd steamroller over me and flatten me into being the sort of person you want me to be.'

'I want you just as you are,' he said softly, his fingers caressing her soft chin. 'Just exactly the way you are, Marcy.' And he bent his head forward to kiss her, so gently, so softly, that the kiss was over in a second or two, but she was left with an indelible impression that in that second he had possessed her, taken her without a struggle, leaving the mark of his ownership on her almost visibly.

'Don't do it, Randal,' she whispered imploringly.

He gave her an odd little smile. 'If you really wanted to get away you could, Marcy,' he told her tolerantly. 'There are no bars on the windows, no locks on the doors. All you have to do is walk away.'

'But . . .' her voice was husky, uncertain, 'you—you won't let me . . .'

'How can I stop you?' he asked gently. 'Everything I do is with your consent, Marcy.'

She stared at **him,** shaking her head. 'No!'

At that instant Sim knocked on the door and put his head round it, glancing swiftly across the room at them, taking in the intimate closeness of their two bodies, the clearly intimate conversation which was taking place. 'Sorry to interrupt . . . you all right, Marcy?'

'Yes, thank you, Sim,' she said, flushing, nervously

aware of Randal watching the two of them.

'Good. You look better. I'm afraid the press is hanging around outside. You'll have a problem getting to your car, Mr Saxton—the street is packed with people.'

Randal frowned. 'Blast!'

As he stared, thoughtfully, at Sim there was a knocking on the back window of the room, and a small black face peered at them. Marcy got up, laughing, and opened the window. 'Wesley!'

'Marcy, you can come out this way,' he said, strutting proudly. 'You and your man will have to crawl along through the sunflowers to the fence through to Noah Road.' He looked at Sim. 'You go and ring for a taxi to pick them up, Mr. It can be waiting for them when they get there.' He gave Marcy a wide grin. 'I've thought of a good way of distracting their attention while you get away. Me and Dost are going to snatch one of the cameras and scarper, then while they're all running after us you can sneak out. Wait for five minutes, then go.' He winked at her. 'Good luck, Marcy.'

'Wesley,' she said, alarmed. 'You'll get into trouble.'

'We'll drop the camera round the corner of Crancy Alley,' he said, indulgently. 'Don't you worry. Most of them reporters are out of condition. They'll never catch me and Dost.'

He had slipped out of the room before she could protest further. She groaned. 'Wesley is a genius, but I'm terrified of what's going to become of him.'

'He sounds as if he's going to be a Napoleon of

crime,' Randal commented in amusement. 'A sharp-witted boy.'

She looked at him eagerly. 'Oh, if only he could find somewhere to go where he could put his talent to work properly,' she said, her eyes sweet. 'Randal . . .'

'No,' he said firmly. 'If you ask me he's having the time of his life. Leave him alone, Marcy.'

'You don't know what I was going to say,' she protested, a sharp disappointment in her voice.

'I'm beginning to recognise the crusading instinct in you,' he said drily.

Her eyes challenged. 'And you don't like it, Randal?'

A strange look came into his face and he made a wry grimace. 'We'll talk about your Wesley later, Marcy,' he said, conceding defeat.

His eyes on his watch, he said, 'His five minutes is up. Over the windowsill with you, Marcy.' He looked at Sim. 'Ring for that damned taxi now'

Sim vanished from the room, and Marcy slithered over the windowsill, dropping to the ground lightly, crouching among the waist-high weeds. A moment later Randal joined her. 'This way,' she whispered, crawling between the thick stems of the sunflowers. Randall glanced with sardonic dismay at his expensive suit, then, with a sigh, followed her.

The trek through the great, topheavy flowers seemed to him to be endless. Marcy crawled without seeming to feel the strain on her back and knees and once looked round at him, dancing amusement in her green glance, as she took in his dry expression.

At last they pushed their way through the broken

fence on the Noah Road side of the garden just as
Sim, in a broken-down white hire car, drew up, wav-
ing to them to jump in to the back of the car. 'My
cousin, Gary,' he explained, pointing to the long-
haired dark young driver, who grinned round at them.
The car drew up two roads away and Sim got out. He
came round to the window beside Marcy, who let it
down and smiled at him affectionately.

'You'll be in touch, Marcy?' he asked her, his eyes
on her small face.

She nodded. 'Sim, you must be on the committee.
We'll see you soon to talk about how it's all to be
arranged.'

'Right,' he said, stepping back.

Gary drove on and Marcy turned to wave at Sim's
tall, distinguished figure, then sat back, aware of
Randal's watchful gaze. 'Where to, Guv?' Gary
asked him, half turning.

Randal gave him the address and a few moments
later Gary dropped them at the white façade of the
house. Walters opened the door to them, a peculiar
look of glazed incredulity on his pouched face. As
they passed him, Marcy looked at him in puzzled
quiry. 'What's wrong, Mr Walters?'

'Walters, Miss,' he begged, in a strangled voice.

Randal threw his butler a flat glance. 'Bring some
tea to the drawing-room, Walters. Miss Marcy would
like some of Anatole's almond gateau.'

'Certainly, sir,' said Walters, but he had that
harried look on his face, and Randal gave him an
irritated, impatient glance.

'Well, what is it, Walters?'

'There was a news story on the radio, sir,' Walters murmured in an agonised voice.

'Oh, dear,' Marcy muttered.

Randal gave her a quelling look. 'About myself and Miss Marcy?'

Walters lifted a pair of appalled eyes to his face. 'Yes, sir.'

'Well?' Randal's mouth was sardonic. 'Aren't you going to congratulate me, Walters?'

Walters looked at him and then at Marcy, gulping like a stranded fish. 'Certainly, sir,' he mumbled. 'Congratulations, sir, miss.' Marcy watched as he tottered towards the baize door.

'Poor Mr Walters! He looks quite stunned.'

'Stop calling him Mr,' said Randal. 'He's my butler. You call him Walters—that's his title.'

'He isn't my butler,' Marcy said defiantly. 'I call him what I like.'

'Oh, God,' Randal muttered with a look of maddened impatience. 'Come in here, you infuriating child, before I go out of my mind!'

Marcy let him pull her into the drawing-room, and there, before she could grasp his purpose, he lifted her into his arms and sat down with her on the couch and began to kiss her hungrily, his hands cradling her head as if she were the child he called her.

'This is getting to be a habit of yours,' she said reprovingly, moving her mouth aside to escape him. 'I don't know what's the matter with you.'

He groaned. 'No, I know you don't. That's what's

driving me insane.' He looked down into her face searchingly. 'Marcy, I'm in a painful dilemma. Help me.'

Puzzled alarm filled her face. 'Of course,' she said quickly. 'What do you want me to do?'

'I'm a man of thirty-two who's fallen madly in love with a child,' he said softly, watching her. 'You're so good at crusading, Marcy. Crusade for me. What am I going to do about it?'

Her eyes grew very bright, her face flushing. 'Randal, don't make jokes about things like that.'

'I'm not joking,' he said. 'I'm in deadly earnest. I fell in love with you at first sight. You dropped down on me like a ton of bricks from that tree, knocking all the breath out of me, and I've felt the impact ever since.'

She sat upright on his lap, gazing at him in stupefaction. She had felt uneasy about him from the first. She had laughed at him, made fun of him, liked him. Now she was quite unable to take her eyes off his hard, handsome face.

'Randal,' she said shakily. 'I . . . I don't know what to say to you. If you're serious . . .'

'Utterly,' he assured her.

'You've only known me for two days!'

'I fell all the way in the first two minutes,' he said blithely.

'Oh,' she said. She looked away, frowning. 'Randal, I've never even had a boy-friend.'

'Good,' he said, satisfaction in his face.

It made her laugh. 'In fact, you're the only man who's ever kissed me the way . . .' She broke off, blushing. 'The—the way you kiss me.'

'Even better,' he said.

'Stop looking like a cat who's stolen the cream,' she snapped, affronted.

'That's how I feel,' he admitted. His arms pulled her backwards suddenly until she fell against his shoulder, in the position she had been in before, and she looked up at him crossly.

'Randal, stop it!'

'Oh, Marcy,' he said thickly. 'I can't . . .' And he began kissing her again, his hands caressing her thick mop of bright hair, his mouth gentle and warm and exciting.

When the door opened and Walters came in, wheeling a tea trolley, she pulled herself upward, bright pink, and sat down sedately beside him on the couch. Walters, looking like a man suffering acute shock, hurriedly departed.

'Shall I pour?' Marcy asked him, her face averted.

'Yes, please,' said Randal, leaning back with a faint sigh. 'I suppose we must have tea.'

There was a banging at the door. Marcy jumped. Randal laid a hand on her knee, calming her. 'Walters won't let a soul into the house,' he assured her.

She heard voices, then the closing of the front door, and Walters appeared, his face blank. 'The press, sir. I told them you and the young lady had gone to Somerset to stay with Lady Anne.'

'Quick thinking, Walters,' Randal said approvingly.

Walters withdrew.

'Lady Anne?' asked Marcy, cutting herself a slice of rich cream gateau. 'Do you want some of this gorgeous cake, Randal?'

'No, thank you,' he said in distaste, eyeing with amazement the size of her slice. 'How do you contrive to keep so thin? You eat enormous meals.'

'Sheer luck,' she said. 'I suppose I'll have to diet when I'm older, but at the moment I'm always hungry.'

'So I've noticed,' he said.

'Who is Lady Anne?' she asked, returning to her question.

'My godmother,' he said. 'You'll love her.' He gave her a quick, amused grin. 'And she'll adore you. I'll take you down to see her tonight.'

'Tonight?' Her eyebrows rose. 'Randal, I'm going back to Paradise Street to start the project, remember.'

'The people there can handle that,' he said.

'It's my house,' she protested.

'You want them to have it, don't you?' he asked. 'Let them decide what they want done with it.'

She stared at him, munching cake. When her mouth was empty, she said, 'But, Randal . . .'

'I thought you believed it should be done democratically,' he said.

'I do!'

'Then let democracy work. If you go down there pushing them in one direction or another it's going to be your project instead of theirs. This Sim of yours can see that it's fair and above board,' he ended a little drily.

Marcy finished her cake, eyeing the rest of it with greedy regret. 'I'd better not have another slice.'

'No, you'd better not,' he said. 'Drink your tea and let's get back to where we were before.'

Her mouth set mutinously. 'Randal, I want to talk to you very seriously . . .'

'Oh, very well,' he said, leaning back. 'What now? Not Wesley?'

'No,' she said, shaking her mop of wild curls. 'Randal, this autumn I'm going to start at drama school. I want to be an actress, if I can, or at least teach drama.'

'Good God,' he exclaimed, gazing at her. 'An actress!'

'So you see why I can't take you seriously, don't you?' she ended gravely.

Randal's eyes were charged with violent electricity. 'Oh, can't you?' he asked, and the ruthless hands took possession of her, sweeping her across his lap again, while he bent his head to find her soft mouth.

Marcy felt a strange beating, pulsing excitement begin to grow inside her as she felt the demanding pressure of the hard mouth. Oh, no, she thought wildly, beginning to struggle. I want him to . . . I can't . . . Her arms flew up in movements which lacked direction, and without her volition closed around his neck. Innocently, awkwardly, her pink lips parted and she groaned almost inaudibly as she began to return his kisses, her hands jerkily caressing the muscled hardness of his neck, the wiry strands of dark hair which seemed so rough against her own white fingers.

Drowning in novel sensations, she told herself to snap out of it, and her hands unlocked from around his neck, moving down to push at his chest, driving him away from her. They had as much effect upon him as a fly might upon an elephant. The long hands which controlled her head, forcing it to remain beneath his kiss, did not even bother to move to stop her frantic little struggles. Gasping, breathing hard, she twined a finger around one of the buttons on his shirt, incoherently begging him to stop.

The button slid undone. She felt the warm naked flesh beneath the open shirt and a sudden tension came into her body. Randal seemed unaware, kissing her deeply, tenderly, his fingers moving constantly over her hair, her cheeks, her ears. Marcy undid another button and slid her hand inside his shirt, feeling the steady hard beat of his heart against her palm. A flood of heated colour swept over her whole body. She was dumbfounded by the way she was feeling, by the things she wanted to do. Slowly she undid all the buttons on his shirt and began to stroke the rough, muscled chest with curious, exploratory fingers.

She had never experienced curiosity about a man's body before, but now she felt an acute, aching need to know all the things her fingers were telling her . . . the rough, dark hair on his skin sending shivers down her spine, the feel of muscle and sinew beneath that skin, the hard bony ribs beneath the chest, the flat midriff which her fingertips searched over slowly.

Randal lifted his mouth at last, his lids almost heavy as he looked down into her eyes. 'Now tell me you can't take me seriously,' he said thickly.

Marcy stared back at him, her mouth dry. 'I . . . I . . .' Her stammered reply brought mockery into his face. He put both hands over her small fingers, pressing them hard into the naked skin of his chest.

Someone knocked on the door at that moment, making her jump in startled alarm.

Randal held her hands under his, smiling at her teasingly. 'I told you, Walters will keep everyone out,' he said.

'He may come in,' she stammered. She looked at the bare brown chest with flushed cheeks. 'Randal, do up your shirt!'

His eyes mocked her. 'You undid it, wanton,' he said softly. 'You do it up.'

She blushed, bending her head, and hurriedly began to do up his buttons, but before she had got halfway through the task the door behind her opened and someone rushed into the room, saying sharply, 'Randal, what the hell is all this about an engagement?' Halfway through the sentence the voice faltered, but carried on, watching the slight body of the girl who lay across Randal's lap, quite obviously doing up his shirt.

Randal's face was bland as he met the newcomer's stare over the bright mop of Marcy's tousled hair. 'Hallo, Julia,' he said coolly. His arm tightened around Marcy as she attempted to get up, forcing her to stay put unless she cared to make an undignified and probably useless struggle for freedom.

Marcy abandoned her attempts both to get off his lap and to do up his shirt. She turned a very flushed, fevered gaze upon the new arrival, who was staring back at her in utter incredulity.

As Marcy looked at her, she sensed sharply that the other woman was deeply angry. There were ice floes in the grey eyes, a bitter hardness about the smooth, intelligent face. Marcy saw a woman of Randal's age, with sleek dark hair and a well-groomed body, a chic clothes sense and an air of assured confidence, but beneath all these things the fact which struck her deepest was the other woman's burning anger.

'Marcy,' Randal said calmly, 'this is Julia Hume, one of the directors of Saxtons. Julia is a legal expert and has a brain like a razor. Julia, this is Marcy, my fiancée.'

Marcy smiled politely at the other woman. Was Randal blind, she asked herself, not to see that Julia was almost sick with jealousy as she looked at them? Then she thought, in a sudden and totally new instinct of jealousy herself, just how well does he know this woman?

CHAPTER FIVE

MARCY was forced to admire Julia's ability to control and disguise her temper. Even as she realised just how badly Julia felt, a shutter seemed to fall down over the other woman's face, and a whimsical smile appeared, a calm, indulgent smile intended more for her benefit, she sensed, than for Randal. 'So you're the little girl from Paradise Street,' she said in what on the surface sounded a friendly voice. Her grey eyes glanced fleetingly at Randal, then back at Marcy. 'Well, I'm fascinated to meet you at last. You've been giving us all a lot of headaches at Saxtons. I was beginning to get really worried about the drain of money the delay was costing us. I might have known I could trust Randal to cut the Gordian knot with one deft blow!' Her laughter had a melodic, artificial sound. 'I'm awed with admiration, Randal.'

Marcy slowly leaned her head back against Randal's half bare chest, her cheek resting on the dark hair on his brown skin. 'He turned a massive defeat into a magnificent victory,' she murmured softly, her mouth curving into a provocative smile. She let her bright head swivel to look up into his face, her eyes veiled by their bright-tipped lashes. 'Didn't you, darling?'

She felt Randal's hand tighten round her body. His face was bland, though, as he said smilingly, 'The

117

Campion Project will be a credit to Saxtons, I'm sure.'

Julia swept a glance over the tea things. 'Feeding little Marcy rich cream cake isn't very sensible, Randal. I'm sure at her age it can only lead to spots and the need to diet. I remember when I was an adolescent I was always terrified of eating anything fattening.'

'Marcy doesn't need to worry,' Randal returned. 'Her skin is as clear as a baby's and she's so small I can get both hands round her waist . . .' He demonstrated, his spread fingers just touching.

'Good lord,' Julia admired, smiling patronisingly. 'So you can—she must be as thin as a boy.'

To Marcy's startled surprise and irritation Randal's long hands moved softly upward to rest just beneath the small rise of her breasts, their touch openly intimate and possessive.

'A boy?' Randal repeated, smiling. 'Oh, I hardly think so.'

Marcy felt a pang of real pity as she saw Julia's uncontrollable, wincing jealousy. The other woman turned away, almost stumbling. 'Well, as the incredible news is true, I'll be off,' she said thickly. 'I hate to intrude on newly betrothed lovers.'

'Goodbye, Julia,' Randal said smoothly.

Marcy said nothing. She was too weak, too moved by pity. The door closed, and she swung off Randal's lap in a sharp movement, turning to look down at him with eyes which did not hold any liking. He lay back, slowly doing up his shirt, watching her shrewdly. They both heard the front door slam behind Julia, and the house grew silent.

'Don't waste any of that spilling compassion of yours for Julia,' he said crisply. 'You don't understand the situation, Marcy, and you have a tendency to leap to conclusions.'

'I may not understand the situation, but I have eyes,' Marcy said quietly.

'You can't always trust what you see,' Randal told her.

'She was ill with jealousy!' Marcy flung at him.

He shrugged. 'I won't dispute that.'

'Then why did you deliberately make it worse?'

His eyes were ice-cold. 'For good reasons.'

'What were they, Randal? The pleasure you were getting out of making her feel pain?'

He sat up abruptly, his lean body instinct with temper. 'No, Marcy. Are you deaf? Julia was trying to belittle you all the time she was here, trying to make you sound like a . . .'

'An adolescent,' Marcy nodded. 'That's what I am, Randal.'

Their eyes met. There was temper in his blue ones, a cool assessment in hers.

'You were hurting Julia because your own mind secretly tells you the same things,' she told him. 'I'm much too young for you. I don't fit into your world. Julia does.'

'I don't want Julia,' he said harshly. 'I never have. And if you're under the impression that she's in love with me, think again. Julia is a clever, ambitious, intelligent woman, but I doubt if she's ever been in love in her life. Jealousy in her is not associated with love. It only means that she coveted the position of being my wife.' He stood up and caught her thin shoulders, shaking her. 'Give me some credit, Marcy. I'm not a fool. Julia has been hanging around giving me broad hints for years. If I had wanted a suitable, very presentable wife she's been there, but I didn't.'

She looked up at him, her eyes anxious. 'Randal, I don't want to marry you.'

His mouth tightened. 'I'll make you,' he said forcefully. 'I can't let you get away from me, Marcy.'

'What do you want from me?' she asked, bewildered, her eyes filled with alarm and bafflement. 'You're rich. You could have any girl you asked. Why me?'

'God help me, I don't know,' he said with a note of self-derision in his voice. 'You've got into my bloodstream. I want you badly, and I'm going to have you.'

She was terrified of the determined sound of his voice, of the restless acquisitive gleam in the blue eyes. She felt an increasing helplessness in front of his pursuit. Totally inexperienced with men, she had grown up in freedom in Cornwall, almost outside the modern world, plunged suddenly into it at eighteen when she came to London, drowning abruptly in a mad circus of newspaper publicity, intrigue, politics and at last her meeting with Randal. She had not yet felt the fierce touch of passion. Randal's lovemaking had puzzled, alarmed, astonished her. She had begun to feel curiosity, even excitement, under his arousing caresses, but she was very far from being in love with him. Had he been a boy of her own age she might have begun to learn the language of love on a novice level, taking her first junior slopes with nervous excitement. But Randal had tried to sweep her away on the crest of an avalanche, and she was floundering out of her depth, in grave danger of total disaster, and deeply aware of it.

She walked towards the smaller of the pictures of a Dutch landscape and stared sightlessly at the pale colours, the dark trees and neat houses. Randal looked hungrily at her slight body, his face flushed and intent.

'Marry me, Marcy,' he said huskily.

'No,' she said, her voice grave. 'It would be a very stupid thing for us to do.' She looked round at him. 'Randal, leave me alone. I can't cope with all this. But my instinct tells me that I mustn't marry you.'

For a moment there was a conflicting confusion in his face, a darkness in his eyes, a hard flush on his cheeks. She could feel the fight going on inside him. His hands clenched by his sides and he breathed erratically as if he were running a hard race.

Then slowly he visibly got control and his hands slowly unclenched. After a pause, he said levelly, 'Then what are you going to do, Marcy?'

'Go to drama school in the autumn,' she said. 'Have fun. Learn about myself and other people.' She looked appealingly at him. 'I've got a lot to learn, Randal. And I want to learn it.'

He breathed deeply. 'And until then I suggest you go to Somerset and stay with my godmother,' he said. 'I want you out of London for a while, Marcy, while the fuss blows over here. You can't go back to

Paradise Street until the whole thing is a dead nine-day's wonder. Will you stay in Somerset until the autumn?'

She smiled at him. 'Thank you, I'd love to.'

'Then I'll drive you down tonight,' he said.

'Tonight?' She looked surprised. 'So soon?'

Randal's mouth dented self-satirically. 'Your presence here under my roof does appalling things to my self-control, Marcy,' he said.

She flushed. 'Oh!'

He came over to her and took her head between his hands, kissing her mouth very softly. 'Your very innocence tempts me beyond belief,' he murmured. 'Haven't you ever looked out of a window at newly fallen snow and felt an urgent desire to rush out and run through it? I'm accustomed to getting my own way, my darling. I'm well aware that you're totally inexperienced and unawakened, and I badly want to be the man who wakes the sleeping beauty with a kiss.' His eyes rested on her pink mouth longingly. 'Oh, Marcy, don't let someone else come between us. I'll wait as patiently as I can, but say now that you belong to me.'

'Don't ask me to make promises I can't keep,' she whispered, her brows uneasy.

He groaned. 'Oh, God, why are you so damned honest?' He pushed her away. 'You'd better choose some more clothes from Anthea's room. Aunt Anne will be amazed if you arrive just in the clothes you stand up in, and those jeans of yours won't pass down in Somerset.'

'I can't take your sister's clothes,' she protested.

He gave her an infuriated look. 'You pig-headed child! Very well, I'll damned well choose some of them and get Walters to pack them for you. As soon as it's dark we'll go. I'll ring for a chauffeur to collect my car from Paradise Street and bring it round here.'

She laughed. 'How easily your life can be managed, Randal. Money really does smooth the way, doesn't it?'

'It helps,' he agreed drily.

'Was Julia telling the truth? Has the Paradise Street business cost you a lot of money?'

He grimaced. 'I doubt if you could conceive how much.'

She watched him. 'What were you doing, Randal, buying me?'

He laughed sardonically. 'Apparently I couldn't even do that.'

'I'm sorry,' she said, pitying him.

Randal looked at her with brief irritation. 'Don't look at me in that way, Marcy. I'm not one of your lame ducks.'

'I know you aren't,' she said cheerfully. 'This take-over bid has failed, but I'm sure your next one will be successful.'

His eyes narrowed at her. 'What's that supposed to mean?'

'Randal, I'll be at drama school for years. You'll find someone else, someone more suitable.'

Randal muttered under his breath, and Marcy laughed. 'Don't huff like the big bad wolf, Randal!'

He gave her a sharp smile. 'Be careful, Marcy. One

day I'll come and blow your house right down and gobble you up unmercifully.'

'The little pigs escaped,' she pointed out. 'It was the wolf who came to a sticky end.'

'I read different books,' he assured her. 'In my version the big bad wolf wins hands down.'

She laughed, feeling a great liking for him. He looked at her abruptly, and she could feel exactly what he was feeling, and a hot colour came into her cheeks, making her turn away.

He turned on his heel and left the room. Marcy sat down on the couch, feeling breathless. She tried to make sense out of her own confused feelings. She liked Randal. She had liked him on sight. There was empathy between them, a natural, instinctive understanding, so that she could sense his thoughts and even his feelings, although she often found them puzzling. She felt easy and comfortable with him except when that look came into his face. She had found him kind, funny, protective . . . yet there was always that look, a curious, hungry look, as if he were sometimes in need of something she was not giving him.

He was attractive. When he kissed her and stroked her hair she felt a pleasant, warm feeling. Her parents had never been demonstrative towards her as a child. Caresses were almost unknown to her, and she found Randal's made her warmly languid, as if they made her bones melt, leaving her helpless in his arms. She was deeply curious about him, curious about how he felt, and how he made her feel, but she felt as if he had presented her with a jigsaw puzzle she could not solve.

Was she falling in love with him? Was that the explanation of the odd sensations he aroused in her?

She recalled the moment when she had been swinging upside down in the tree in the garden at Paradise Street, and he had appeared so suddenly. She had looked at him, her hair tumbling backwards, and had lost her balance and fallen, to be caught in Randal's strong, hard arms.

Everything had begun at that moment. From the first instant she had felt an immediate, irresistible attraction towards him, knowing that he was someone she could like immensely.

She felt as if, like Alice, she had fallen down and down a great dark well at that moment, taking Randal with her, and now she had to regain her balance. The last two days had been a whirl of confused experience. She had felt more, experienced more, in those two days than ever in her life before, but she could make no sense out of any of it. She needed time, and so did Randal, if they were not to make a disastrous mistake.

They drove to Somerset in the warm dark night, rarely talking. Randal seemed abstracted, and Marcy was relieved that he was not in the mood to talk, since she was facing the fact that soon she would say good-bye to him, and finding the idea oddly unpleasant.

As they left the outer reaches of suburbia behind they drove into an English countryside still marked with the vestiges of more ancient times—barrows made smooth eruptions on the dark horizon of the hills, lonely houses with thatched roofs and black and white timbering appeared occasionally, there were the misty outlines of sheep on the cold downs. Now and then another car passed them, headlights glaring. Otherwise they drove on through a silent land.

Marcy grew sleepy and slid back against the seat, her head drooping. Randal glanced down at her, pushed her gently sideways so that his arm could just surround her, and drove on, feeling the soft weight of her slender body against his side with a sensation of silent possession which made his whole face soften.

He turned into a white gate, propped open by a ragged stone, and drove on along a long, broad lane, with lime trees darkly lacing overhead, towards the distant outline of a long, white house.

Parking at the back of the house, he detached himself from Marcy and got out, then bent forward, lifting her into his arms, his hands convulsively holding her close for a second, his face buried in her soft hair. Then he straightened and walked towards the back door of the house. It opened as he reached it and a thin old woman in a flowered cotton dressing-gown peered at him, light shedding a circle around her.

'Randal!' whispered a voice, staring at the frail body in his arms. 'Come in.'

Randal passed her, kissing her wrinkled, soft cheek as he did so. 'Hallo, Chumble . . .'

In the same whispered voice the old woman said, 'You'd better bring her upstairs. I've put her in the room Anthea uses.'

Randal followed her erect, thin figure up a flight of winding wooden stairs and along a corridor into a bedroom. Gently, with reluctance, he lowered Marcy's sleeping body on to the bed. She stirred, waking as the warmth of his closeness left her, and stared upward, blinking sleepily. 'Oh!' she yawned, then came awake suddenly, and started up, staring around.

'I'll help her get into bed, Randal,' said the old woman briskly. 'I've got a kettle on. Go down and make some tea.'

'I've got to drive straight back to London,' he said briefly. 'I just want to say goodbye to Marcy, Chumble.'

The old woman eyed him almost reprovingly, then nodded. She went out and Randal thrust his hands into his pockets, looking down at Marcy expressionlessly.

She drew her knees up and put her arms around them, almost defensively, her chin on them, looking at him.

'It's a long drive back to London. Do you think you should do the journey twice in one night?'

'Never mind that,' he said. 'I have an appointment tomorrow at three. I'll get some sleep tomorrow morning.' He sighed deeply. 'Now listen to me, Marcy. I'll see that everything goes well at Paradise Street. Trust me.'

'I do,' she said simply.

He looked at her green eyes, then at her weary mouth. 'In two days I'm due to fly to New York and then to Canada,' he told her. 'I've got a round of talks to get through over the next fortnight, then after that I've got to go to Japan. I can't get back to England for almost a month.'

Marcy felt a coldness on her skin, but she smiled. 'I hope you enjoy your trip,' she said politely.

His mouth twisted bitterly. 'Oh, God, Marcy, I've never wanted to go anywhere less!'

She felt a strange compassion for him, and held out her arms in a childlike gesture of affection. Randal sat down and she put her arms around his neck, stroking the back of his dark head.

He looked into her green eyes, his face lined with weariness. 'Don't forget me while I'm gone,' he said huskily.

She leaned forward and kissed his tired mouth with tenderness. 'I couldn't do that, Randal.'

His lips awoke under her softness and he began to kiss her in that hungry way of his, his hands trembling as he held her. Marcy was so tired. The warmth and comfort of his kisses made her languid. She slowly sank back on the pillows and Randal lay, softly kissing her, his hands moving over her restlessly. She was yieldingly responsive, her brain too tired to think, and barely noticed when Randal's hands began to move over her lace blouse, undoing her buttons, sliding in to find her warm smooth skin. Her eyes were drowsily closed, her slenderness relaxed, as he slid his mouth down her white throat and began to kiss her bare shoulders. 'Oh, God, Marcy, I love you,' he groaned, his mouth hot on her skin.

The door opened at that instant and the old woman in the floral dressing-gown came into the room, carrying a tray which bore a cup of tea and some plain biscuits. She stopped, looking deeply shocked, and Randal sat up, his face darkly flushed.

'Randal! What do you think you're doing?' The old woman had a sharp, angry note in her reedy voice.

Randal looked confused. He glanced at Marcy, who, very pink, was pulling her open blouse together with trembling fingers. 'I must go. Marcy, I'll write to you. I . . .' His voice cut off as if he found it hard to speak. He looked at the old woman. 'Chumble, look after her.'

The old woman probed his face with faded but still sharp eyes. 'I'll look after her, Randal,' she said, in a softer tone.

Randal nodded, then bent, lifting both Marcy's small hands to his mouth.

She felt his mouth burn on her palms, felt him hold them both briefly against his cheek, then he released them and walked out of the room.

Chumble put down the tray and looked oddly at Marcy. 'Drink your tea, miss. I'll be back when I've seen Mr Randal off.'

Marcy sat, sipping her tea, her blouse done up again. She was still feeling fluttering butterflies in her stomach after the moments when she and Randal had kissed.

The old woman came back and watched as she finished her tea and sat up straight. 'Now, off to bed with you,' she said briskly. 'I'm Chumble. I was Randal's nanny when he was a little boy. My real name is Miss Chumley, but he could never say it.'

Marcy smiled, that quick, radiant childlike smile

which had first made Randal's heart stop. 'It suits you,' she said. 'It's a lovely name.'

Chumble's face softened further. 'How old are you, miss?' she asked, helping Marcy deftly with her gnarled old hands to get undressed.

March looked at her, a slight wry smile on her mouth. 'I'm just eighteen,' she said.

'Eighteen!' Chumble's face was dismayed. 'You're nothing but a child!'

Marcy slid out of the black velvet suit and stood in her bra and panties, a slender pale figure, her white skin gleaming. 'I know,' she said. 'I'm too young for him. I've told him that, but Randal is very obstinate.'

Chumble had brought up the case which Randal had had packed for her, and was finding a nightgown. She held it up, a frown on her face.

'It's Anthea's,' Marcy told her. 'Randal said my own clothes wouldn't do for Lady Anne.'

Chumble gave her a quick, surprised look, but said nothing, pushing her into the white wisp of silk. Marcy clambered into bed and sat up, hugging her knees, the bright marigold gleam of her head even gaudier above the white silk.

'Walters packed them for me,' she said.

'Walters!' Chumble snorted. 'They'll have to be pressed. He can't pack handkerchiefs.'

Marcy grinned. 'I like him,' she said. 'And Anatole . . . they're both very kind.'

'The bathroom is down the corridor,' said Chumble, ignoring the statement. 'Breakfast is at nine. Lady Anne rides first thing in the morning, and has a late breakfast. When you've recovered from the journey you could ride with her.'

'I don't ride horses,' said Marcy. 'I've never ridden.'

Chumble looked disgusted. 'You'll learn,' she said firmly. She moved to the door. 'Good night, miss.'

'My name is Marcy, Chumble,' said Marcy softly.

Chumble's thin lips twitched. 'Marcy . . . what sort of name is that? You were never christened Marcy.'

'Marcia,' Marcy grimaced. 'But that's hateful! Call me Marcy, Chumble.'

'Just as you like, miss,' said Chumble stiffly.

Marcy's bright gamin smile shone out again. 'Was Randal a good little boy?'

'A wicked one,' said Chumble, softening against her will. 'His mother doted on him.'

'Walters said it hit him hard when his mother died.'

'Walters knows nothing about it,' said Chumble jealously.

'Didn't it?'

Chumble met her probing green eyes with reluctance. 'I think it nearly broke his heart,' she admitted. She looked at Marcy oddly. 'She wasn't unlike you, miss. There's a portrait of her in the library. She was Lady Anne's cousin, you know, and they were very close. When Lady Anne dies she'll leave the portrait to Randal in her will, she says, but she won't part with it until she goes. She was very fond of Miss Natalie.'

'Natalie,' murmured Marcy. 'What a lovely name.'

Chumble straightened. 'Now, when you've been to

the bathroom, off to bed and get some sleep. You look worn out.'

'Yes, Chumble,' Marcy said submissively.

'Goodnight,' said Chumble, unmoved by her submission. She went out and Marcy made a little face at the door. Clearly, Chumble was no easy proposition. One had to build respect in her before she would view one with anything but disapproval. She slipped out to the bathroom, washed and cleaned her teeth, then went back to bed and fell asleep almost at once out of sheer exhaustion.

When she awoke it was to find the whole room flooded with bright sunlight. She lay against the pillows, watching the blaze of sunlight on the polished furniture of the room, admiring the clarity of the light. Somewhere she could hear the bleat of sheep, a constant sound which had comfort in it. The sky beyond the window was a blue so soft and bright it made her suddenly eager to get up. She sprang out of bed and found a silk negligee which matched the nightgown hanging from a hook on the door, where Chumble had neatly placed it the night before.

Sliding into it, she went out to the bathroom and took a swift shower. Returning, fresh and lively, she looked through the clothes which Walters had packed, and chose a very simple cream linen dress which, although it was clearly exquisitely cut, had a clean line which satisfied her.

Lucky Anthea, she thought, brushing her mop of wild hair until it had a sheen to it. It must be wonderful to have so many clothes. She wondered what sort of girl Randal's sister would be, her brow wrinkled curiously. Would she ever meet her? It would be rather fun if they liked each other.

Chumble suddenly appeared and gave her a long, considering look, nodding approvingly.

'That's a very nice dress, miss,' she said. 'Your breakfast is ready. Lady Anne just got back from her ride. She's changing in her room now.'

Will she like me? Marcy wanted to ask her, but she said nothing of the sort, her small face rather pale as she followed Chumble down the wide main staircase into a white-painted hall.

Breakfast was laid in the morning room, Chumble informed her, opening a smooth oak door. Marcy found herself in a square room flooded with sunshine, and Chumble indicated a seat at the pleasant round table. 'Lady Anne will be down directly. Will you have fruit juice or porridge?'

Marcy was starving. 'Porridge, please,' she said.

It was deliciously creamy, she decided, sprinkling it with sugar and flooding it with milk. She made a moat in the thick texture of the cereal and watched as the milk filled it. Chumble stood behind her, staring over her shoulder.

There were brisk steps and Marcy, a mouthful of creamy porridge in her mouth, glanced round apprehensively, meeting a pair of clear blue eyes set in a weatherbeaten brown face, all angles and shrewd appraisal.

'Good morning,' said the newcomer, extending a roughened hand. 'I'm Anne Carlew. You must be Marcy Campion.'

Marcy took her hand, hastily gulping down porridge, and the other woman glanced from her flushed face to her half eaten bowl of porridge with a peculiar expression. 'It's very kind of you to have me to stay,' said Marcy, when she could speak.

'I hope you enjoy your visit,' Lady Anne said, sitting down. 'Porridge, Chumble.'

'Yes, my lady,' said Chumble, placing the porridge in front of her.

Lady Anne concentrated on her food and Marcy obediently did the same. Her empty bowl was whisked away.

'Poached egg on toast or egg and bacon, miss?' mumbled Chumble.

'Egg and bacon,' said Marcy. 'Thank you, Chumble.'

The meal proceeded in silence, then, as she drank a very large cup of very strong tea, Lady Anne leaned back and studied Marcy with blue eyes which reminded Marcy strongly of Randal's eyes.

'So you're the girl from Paradise Street,' Lady Anne said with a sudden smile. 'You aren't what I expected.'

Marcy looked impish. 'What did you expect?'

'Difficult to say,' grunted the other woman. She was in her late fifties, Marcy decided. She had a hard, tough face with skin like tanned leather and a strong, decided mouth. Randal might one day have a face like that, she thought, shivering a little. He had that ruthless, determined expression already.

'So you're going to marry Randal,' Lady Anne went on.

Marcy made no reply. She did not like to deny it directly, yet she was wary of agreeing. Lady Anne looked at her from under thick brows.

'Aren't you?'

'We've only known each other for three days,' said Marcy. 'I don't think that's long enough.'

Lady Anne looked past her at Chumble, raising a curious eyebrow. Chumble stood, with her gnarled, pale blue hands linked at her waist, her expression guarded.

'Well, never mind,' said Lady Anne. 'After breakfast I'll take you on a tour of the place. Like horses, do you?'

'I like animals,' Marcy said. 'But I don't ride.'

For a moment Lady Anne looked at her as if she had said something blasphemous, then she said roughly, 'Well, you'll soon learn. Randal's wife must ride. He loves horses.'

'Walters packed some of Anthea's jodhpurs,' Chumble observed.

Lady Anne nodded. 'There you are, then.'

Randal, thought Marcy wryly, must have intended her to ride, since he had picked out the clothes which Walters had packed. After breakfast she followed Lady Anne into a rectangular drawing-room and looked around it with pleasure and admiration. It was not the elegant, formal sort of room which she had seen in Randal's house. This room was as cosy and homely as her sitting-room at home—the chintz-covered chairs were loose with age, sagging from use; there were ornaments and pictures everywhere, photographs of people, vases of flowers, fringed lamps, little tables, piles of books. The profusion and confusion was comforting.

'What a lovely room,' she said, sighing with relief. She had feared to find herself in grand isolation as she had when she came down to breakfast in Randal's house and looked with horror at the gleaming dining-room.

Lady Anne led her into the next room. It was a library, lined with shelves of books, a dusty cold room after the previous one, but on a wall hung a portrait which drew Marcy's eyes at once. Forgetting Lady Anne, she walked over to it and stared intently at a picture of a very young girl in a simple, beautiful white dress, whose soft dark hair and wide, gentle eyes had a beauty beyond that of feature.

Her slight body had a fragility which was visible, but there was the hint of a smile in the blue eyes which was very touching. Marcy traced hints of Randal in the shape of the features, the colouring, the tantalising smile.

'My cousin Natalie,' said Lady Anne gruffly, behind her.

Marcy turned, her own mouth gently smiling. 'Yes, I recognise the look of Randal.'

Lady Anne stared at her oddly. Her brows levelled out and her eyes softened. 'Humm . . .' she said in a tone like a grumpy bear. 'Come on, then.' She turned and stumped away, and Marcy followed her.

After a brief tour of the house they went out to the stables. They were neat and clean, Marcy noted, three horses peering out at her curiously as they crossed the cobbles towards the stalls.

An old man in a flat cap with a yardbroom in his hand came sulkily towards them. 'Yes, m'lady?' His tone defied her to ask him to do anything.

'Just looking, Grimshaw,' said Lady Anne sarcastically. 'Don't mind if we do that, I suppose?'

'I've got a lot to catch up with,' he said in the same sulky tone. 'My back's playing up again, and I've got the muck to shift.'

Lady Anne ignored him. 'You can ride Ladybird tomorrow,' she told Marcy. 'She's safe as houses.'

Marcy looked at the fat, white horse and knew she was not alarmed at the prospect.

'Ladybird don't like going out any more,' Grimshaw said jealously. 'She's too old for work, like me.'

'I'm very light,' Marcy assured him earnestly. 'She'll hardly notice me on her back.' Ladybird looked capable of carrying several girls on her back, indeed, her broad well-filled expanse hugely efficient.

Grimshaw growled at her. 'She's obstinate, is Ladybird.'

'She's lazy,' said Lady Anne derisively. 'She eats too much and doesn't do a stroke. I'll sell her to a knackers' yard if she doesn't pull her socks up.'

Grimshaw's little black eyes looked nasty. 'Hrrr!' He mumbled as he shuffled away, his broom trailing.

Marcy looked at Lady Anne in alarm. 'You've hurt his feelings.'

'Hasn't got any,' said Lady Anne. 'Worked here all his life and thinks he owns the place. Sometimes I have to saddle the damned horse myself because he won't do it. If he had his way, the animals wouldn't do a stroke.' She grinned, watching Grimshaw disappear into the back of the house. 'Now he's gone to pick a row with Chumble. They lead a cat and dog

life downstairs. God, the rows they have! I keep out
of it. If I try to smooth them down they both turn on
me, and life isn't worth living until they get out of
their black mood.'

Marcy looked around the neat stable. 'It must be a
lot of work for him to do. He's rather old.'

'He's pensioned off,' said Lady Anne tartly. 'He's
got his own cottage and enough to live on, but he
refuses to retire. This is his life, poor old Grimshaw,
and he's determined not to let someone else come in
and lay a hand on his stableyard. I'd have some help
for him, but he won't hear of it.'

Marcy looked along the rambling façade of the
house as they strolled round to the front. 'It's a
beautiful house,' she said. 'It must be very hard to
keep clean.'

'Two women from the village do the hard work,'
said Lady Anne. 'Chumble looks after all that.' She
grimaced. 'Like Grimshaw, she refuses to retire. She
wants to feel needed, and, to be honest, she is, here
. . . I'd miss her like hell if she went, and she knows
it. We've been together for years, ever since Randal
and Anthea grew up.'

'Oh, she was Anthea's nanny, too?'

'Oh, yes, she took Anthea from birth. Delighted to,
as well, because by then Randal was at school and
she was bored stiff. Chumble likes to be busy.'

'So do I,' admitted Marcy.

The soft air of the Somerset downs flooded the
façade with light. She sniffed appreciatively. 'It's very
beautiful down here,' she said.

'After London it's heaven,' said Lady Anne. 'Londoner, aren't you?'

Marcy shook her head, smiling. 'Not really. I was born and brought up in Cornwall. My father and mother lived there all their lives.'

Lady Anne stared at her. 'Campion . . . Cornwall . . .' Her face had a thoughtful frown. 'Whereabouts did you live?'

'A small village called Trebode,' Marcy told her. 'We lived outside it, actually.'

'Trebode,' said Lady Anne. 'Got it . . . Campion! Your father was a naturalist, wasn't he?'

Marcy smiled affectionately. 'Sometimes, yes. He wrote articles for magazines about wild life.'

'Read some of them,' Lady Anne nodded. 'He took some very good photographs of wild birds. I admired them.' She gave Marcy a brisk, approving smile. 'Dead, is he?'

Marcy nodded. 'And my mother – killed in a car crash. Father was very interested in furniture. He was going to an auction at Bodmin when he crashed. Heart attack, they said.'

'Pity,' said Lady Anne. 'I'd like to have met him. So he liked birds and furniture . . . what else did he like?'

Marcy gave a wry smile. 'He liked a lot of things. He spent most of his time reading. He and my mother were much older than parents should be, I think . . . they were already set in their ways when I was born. I think I was a shock to them. I disrupted their comfortable lives, although they were fond of me.

They'd never needed anyone but each other. They were perfectly matched.'

'That's nice,' said Lady Anne. 'Nice for them, I mean.'

Marcy laughed. 'Nice for me, too, in a way. Marriage should be like that, don't you think?'

'And you don't think you and Randal are perfectly matched?' asked Lady Anne with a sudden directness that made Marcy gasp.

Flushing, Marcy said honestly, 'Well, we can't be, can we? Coming from such different backgrounds and being such different ages.'

'The age gap bothers you?' asked Lady Anne.

Marcy met her eyes. 'Doesn't it bother you?'

Lady Anne laughed abruptly. 'It did, but now I'm not so sure. You remind me a little of his mother. Natalie wasn't as open and direct as you are, Marcy. She was shy and rather retiring. But to look at, you have a similar build, and Natalie was always a warm, affectionate creature.' She turned towards the house. 'Come along, Chumble will be waiting to serve luncheon. Are you hungry?'

'I'm always hungry,' Marcy admitted, grinning.

And Lady Anne laughed. 'Good. Come on, then, before Chumble starts to sulk like an old chimney!'

CHAPTER SIX

MARCY's first riding lesson was a disaster. Ladybird, saddled and bridled by Grimshaw with a thunderous expression, stood like a white rock, refusing to move while Marcy helplessly kicked at her fat sides.

'Told you so,' Grimshaw observed in satisfaction, making no attempt to help.

Lady Anne slapped Ladybird crossly with her crop on her haunches, and the fat white horse gave a sideways jump of annoyance, but still refused to budge. Marcy leaned forward, her slender body even more boylike in the biscuit-coloured jodhpurs and white shirt, and whispered coaxingly into Ladybird's backward flicking ears.

'Dig your knees in,' Lady Anne suggested.

Marcy pushed her knees into the soft white back, her small hands gripping the reins, and sulkily Ladybird turned to sneer at her.

Lady Anne grabbed the bridle and walked forward on her own bay mare, yanking at Ladybird's recalcitrant head. Ladybird obstinately lowered her nose and looked immovable.

'You go on,' said Marcy. 'I'll try to get her used to me.'

Grimshaw leaned on an open door, a grim smile on his face. Lady Anne gave him a furious glare but went on ahead. Ladybird flicked her tail irritably, then

141

slowly, sulkily, followed. Lady Anne looked round at Marcy with a grin.

'Make you sick, don't they? Feather-brained animals!'

Suddenly Ladybird began to trot and helplessly Marcy jogged up and down, unable to grasp the rhythm, while Lady Anne bellowed at her to go with the horse, not fight it.

By the time Marcy had grasped exactly how to fit in with the movement, Ladybird had sulkily lapsed back into a walk. Sore, aching, cross, Marcy sat and felt like kicking the fat white back.

On the way back to the house Ladybird broke into a trot again, and after a moment of confusion Marcy began to find herself rising and falling with her mount. Lady Anne gave her an approving smile. 'Better, Marcy, much better,' she said, nodding.

After breakfast Marcy and Lady Anne did some gardening, working in the sunny garden with trowels and wicker baskets, pulling up weeds, pruning, cutting out dead flowers. Chumble had decided, for her own reasons, to serve lunch out in the garden, so they ate salad and cold ham at a white-painted wicker table on the grass, drinking lemonade with it out of a frosted blue jug.

During the afternoon Lady Anne drove in a battered old car over to visit a friend, so Marcy went down to the kitchen and helped Chumble to pot gooseberry jam. Chumble was disconcerted at first, but by the time she had got around to telling Marcy about Randal's obstinate, wicked behaviour as a small boy, she had forgotten her first sullen disapproval, and by the time Lady Anne returned the two of them were happily polishing silver around the kitchen table while the whole room held the warm fruity fragrance of the hot jam.

After dinner Lady Anne got out a tapestry frame and began to work. 'D'you embroider, Marcy?' she asked.

'Mother taught me to do some,' Marcy admitted. She had spent hours with pricked fingers and tangled threads as a child, but at length she had achieved a passable imitation of a tablecloth.

Lady Anne sorted out a piece of oblong linen. 'Why don't you make a traycloth? Peaceful occupation, embroidery.'

Marcy chose a simple heraldic design of a black gryphon on a green base—Lady Anne grinned at her. 'My family crest,' she said. 'Have it on a lot of my things.'

The evening passed peacefully as they sat embroidering while they listened to a record.

In bed that night Marcy sleepily thought of Randal. What was he doing? Was he thinking of her? Or had his absorbing business life already swallowed him up into its maw, removing all traces of her from his mind? Beyond her window the country silence echoed darkly. She heard the wind whispering through the trees, the distant whistle of a train. What was happening in Paradise Street? Had Sim and Lisa become reconciled? That seemed a world away from here and now. Life was as strange as Lady Anne's tapestry, a mass of loose threads and jumbled colours, contradictory, confused and baffling.

Day after day passed and she became used to the routine of the house. She rode on Ladybird each morning, and found her gradually more malleable. 'She's losing weight, thank God,' said Lady Anne, eyeing Ladybird's white bulk with grim amusement. 'Exercise is doing her good.'

Sometimes if Lady Anne were busy Marcy went to the stables and helped Grimshaw with his work, despite his grumbled protests that he didn't need it.

She worked in the garden, enjoying herself enormously as she weeded or planted out. She helped Chumble in the kitchen, cooking, cleaning, washing up. She dusted and tidied the rooms. She read some of the piles of books Lady Anne left lying about, enjoying the illustrations in some of the natural history tomes. She ate with her usual eager appetite, and she did her embroidery.

Lady Anne took her to the village nearby and they sorted old clothes for a jumble sale. They went to church on Sunday and she listened with amusement to Lady Anne shouting out the hymns roughly in her penetrating voice. The bespectacled, smiling vicar shook her hand and accepted an offer of flowers for the altar next week, so she went down later with a large plastic bucket full of cut flowers from the garden.

The small church had some impressive stone monuments, brass plaques glinting in the sunlight. When she had arranged the flowers she walked around the church, her own bright head like brass, as she read the names.

Rainbow light filtered through the stained glass

windows, falling in shifting patterns of brightness
over the pews. The smell of dust and the flowers, the
chill coldness of the stone under her feet, were
nostalgic of her childhood. She went out into the
churchyard with its white tombstones and grey
pigeons and looked curiously along the narrow village
street.

She was turning to make the half mile walk back
to the house when a bright red sports car pulled up
with a jerk beside her, and a grinning, friendly face
appeared over the lowered window.

'Need a lift?' asked the young owner.

Marcy gave him a thoughtful scrutiny. He was in
his twenties, a rather gaudy yellow shirt open at his
slim neck, his eyes full of brown gaiety and reckless-
ness.

'Where to?' she asked.

'Aunt Anne's,' he said mischievously, grinning, a
lock of bronze brown hair falling over his temples,
watching the look of surprise and puzzlement coming
into her eyes.

'Who are you?' she asked, staring at him.

'I'm Perry Horsnall,' he said lightly. 'Randal's
cousin. And you're the mysterious and magical Miss
Marcy Campion who took on the might of the
Saxton Empire and beat them hollow by snatching
their emperor from under their noses.'

Marcy laughed, instantly and childishly. 'You're an
idiot,' she grinned, but she flung her plastic bucket
into the back of the car and climbed into the passenger seat beside him.

He dramatically started the engine and raced away

down the road. Sideways glances inspected her from head to foot in her silky peacock blue shift which, for all its expensive allure, merely enforced the effect of her youth and faint wildness.

'That's Anthea's dress,' he observed. 'I've seen her wear it.'

'Go to the top of the class,' said Marcy. 'Didn't anyone tell you it was rude to make personal remarks?'

'Frequently,' he nodded. 'All the same, how come you're wearing it? She isn't here, is she?'

'No, I think she's still in Switzerland,' Marcy agreed. 'Randal lent some of her clothes to me. He didn't like my own.'

'Not surprised,' said Perry frankly. 'You don't have a London accent. How come you were living in that dump, anyway?'

'You didn't read your papers closely enough,' she said reprovingly. 'My home was in Cornwall. I just inherited the London house.'

'Ah,' he said. 'I've got it. Randal's in Canada, isn't he?'

Marcy flushed. Every day postcards had been arriving with brief, almost remote messages from him, as if they were strangers.

'Yes,' she said quietly. 'He goes on to Japan soon.'

Perry grinned at her. 'I don't believe he's going to marry you. You look about sixteen.'

'I'll tell Chumble how rude you are, and she won't let you have any cake for tea,' she said.

He gave a roar of laughter. 'Get on with Chumble, do you? Oh, lord, that tears it! There's just one person in this world I'm frightened of, and that's Chumble. She gave me nightmares when I was a kid— God, I was glad she wasn't my nanny. When Anthea came to tea Chumble used to look at me as if I was a caterpillar she was going to step on.'

'I can imagine why,' said Marcy. 'You aren't coming to stay, are you?'

'If Aunt Anne lets me,' he said. 'My father sent me with a box of books he found at an auction. Dull old horsy books. She'll love them. It may put her in enough of a good mood to ask me to stay.'

He roared down the drive and pulled up outside the house with a violent jerk. Marcy gave him a frosty glare. 'Thanks for the lift, and in future I'll walk. It's safer.'

She went into the house and he followed her after a moment, staggering under the weight of a huge box of books. Lady Anne appeared, astonished by the sight of him.

'Perry! What on earth are you doing here?'

He gratefully dropped the box and leaned, puffing against the wall. 'For you, Aunt Anne, from Dad with love. Horse books.'

'You're badly out of condition,' Marcy told him. 'You puff worse than Ladybird.'

Lady Anne knelt down and opened the box, exclaiming with delight over the contents. 'How kind of dear Peter to think of me. Good heavens, this one is a very early edition . . .'

'Aunt Anne, can I stay for a day or two?' Perry asked idly. 'I'm on holiday now and I can't afford to go away this year.'

'Of course, dear,' said Lady Anne absently, taking out more of the books. Then she looked up in alarm. 'If Chumble says you can.'

Perry looked alarmed. He gazed at Marcy imploringly. 'You ask Chumble, there's a dear . . . she terrifies me.'

'Ask her yourself,' said Marcy.

Lady Anne was deep in the box of books, so Perry seized Marcy by the arm and marched her towards the kitchen, hissing, 'Don't be a bad sport. She'll say yes if you ask her, and I'm stony broke.'

'Where do you work?' she asked him.

'Where do you think?' he asked gloomily. 'I'm one of the slaves in the Saxton saltmine, but I'm only earning a crust.'

'Which part of the saltmine?' she enquired.

'Legal department,' he said glumly. 'I was fool enough to take a law degree and for my sins I spend all day poring over the most atrociously dull documents under the very stern eye of Miss Julia Hume . . .'

Marcy halted, looking at him sharply. 'Was it her idea you should come down here?'

Perry's open, frank face flushed crimson. 'Oh, lord,' he said in horrified tones. He gave her a gloomy look. 'I suppose now I've let the cat out of the bag with a vengeance. Julia warned me to be casual and cunning . . .' His mouth grimaced. 'You're quick-witted. How on earth did you jump to that conclusion?'

'I've met her,' Marcy explained, 'She detests me.'

'Are you surprised? She's been toiling around after Randal for centuries and you just walked in and pinched him in five minutes,' Perry said. He sighed. 'I suppose bang goes my chance of staying here now.'

'Why not?' said Marcy. 'It makes no difference to me.'

'It doesn't?' He gazed at her in astonishment. 'No,' he said wryly, 'I don't suppose it does. Why Julia imagines any girl would look at me if she could have Randal I don't know.'

Marcy laughed. 'She must be desperate.'

'Oh, thanks,' said Perry, offended. 'I know I'm not exactly Prince Charming, but there's no need to be unpleasant about it.'

'Are you really hard up?' she asked, eyeing his clothes and thinking of his expensive car.

'You'd better believe it. Every penny I earn goes in five minutes, and I somehow seem to get worse. My car eats money and my girl-friends have very expensive tastes.'

'You've got girl-friends?' Marcy mocked.

He grinned. 'Piranhas, all of them. They strip me bare and then vanish.'

'Poor Perry,' she said. 'Come and see Chumble.'

Chumble eyed him distastefully. 'What on earth are you wearing Mr. Perry? It looks like a table-cloth.'

He looked at his eye-catching yellow shirt uneasily. 'It's silk,' he said hopelessly.

'Very vulgar,' said Chumble. 'You wouldn't catch Mr Randal wearing anything like that.'

Marcy perched on the edge of the table. 'He's broke, Chumble,' she told her.

'I'm not surprised. Yellow silk shirts. Well!'

'He wants to stay for a few days,' Marcy added. 'But it will be too much work for you, won't it, even if I help out?'

Chumble looked affronted. 'I'm not in my dotage yet, miss. When I'm senile, I'll tell you so, don't worry. Of course Mr Perry can stay.' She gave him a sharp, reproving look. 'If he behaves himself like a young gentleman.'

'Oh, I will,' Perry promised, beaming.

'Humm,' said Chumble disagreeably.

Perry's presence made a difference at once to Marcy's life. He made a threesome during the morning rides, easily and capably riding the tall, bay gelding which belonged to Randal, and Marcy found him an excellent teacher. When she was not helping around the house and garden, he taught her some easy jumps in a flat meadow at the back of the house, shouting abusively at her when she landed badly, and demonstrating with careless grace exactly how she should do something.

In the evenings, instead of embroidery, she and Perry played cards and quarrelled noisily over them, gambling for matches. Lady Anne ignored their nursery squabbles as she embroidered, but Chumble would come in and eye them broodingly. 'Time for bed, Miss Marcy,' she would announce, as if longing to smack both of them.

Perry took her for rides in his sports car, driving with wild speed around the narrow country lanes, telling her stories about Anthea as a little girl. 'Is she pretty?' Marcy asked, and Perry made a peculiar face.

'She's . . . oh, I don't know. She's Anthea.'

His tone made her laugh. 'You know her better than Randal?'

Perry grimaced. 'Randal's a pirate, a chip off the old block. I wouldn't turn my back on him for a second.' And he told her stories about the founder of the family who had built his fortunes by nefarious, suspected means. 'I know people who think Randal's just a playboy,' he ended grimly. 'They just don't know him. He's ruthless, tough and bloody unpleasant if he gets mad.'

'Yes, I can believe he might be,' Marcy agreed solemnly, her small face filled with thought.

Perry had been at the house for a week when he and Marcy were playing croquet on the old lawn at the back of the house, with the fragrance of the roses filling the warm air, squabbling in their way over the rules of the game.

Marcy threw down her mallet, announcing that she would not play with a cheat any more.

As she stalked away, Perry caught her hand, laughing, 'Pax, Marcy, pax, I won't cheat any more.'

'Liar,' she said, beginning to laugh at the expression of cunning on his face.

Perry bent forward and kissed her lightly. 'Promise,' he said, then he looked down at her, almost curiously. 'You're a very pretty girl, Marcy,' he said, kissing her again, lingeringly.

She stood still under his kiss, wondering why it gave her none of the strange, nervous excitement Randal's kisses gave her. Her wild, marmalade mop of hair blazed in the sunlight above the slightness of her body in the clinging peacock blue silk she wore. Turning, pushing Perry lightly but not disagreeably away, she faced Randal, and felt a sharp plunge of the heart as she saw the look on his face.

Randal was holding a branch of a green-laced lilac tree in his tense hand as he stared at the two young people. He had been watching for a moment or two, long enough to feel the ease and companionship between them, the amiable, carefree friendship which the closeness of their age gave them. He had been childishly jealous of Perry from the first, bitterly envious of his young cousin's ability to meet Marcy on such ground. But when Perry bent to kiss her his whole body had blazed into savage jealousy. He stared at them, narrow-eyed, intentionally menacing, filled with a primitive desire to do something violent.

Perry dragged his feet, flushed and awkward, petrified of his cousin's expression. 'Oh, hallo, Randal . . . welcome back. I . . . I'll go and tell Chumble you're here.' He rushed past him, avoiding meeting the dangerous blue eyes.

Marcy quietly met Randal's glare. He released the branch of the lilac tree and slowly walked over to her. She did not move or look frightened, staring at him almost assessingly.

Randal's long hand lifted her chin. The other carefully brought out a white handkerchief and brushed it across her lips, erasing Perry's kiss firmly.

'What's he doing here?' he asked her tersely.

'Staying for a holiday,' Marcy said steadily.

The long fingers tightened on her chin. 'Was that the first time he'd kissed you?'

Marcy felt a trembling in the pit of her stomach. 'You don't own me, Randal,' she said huskily. 'We agreed that I made you no promises, remember?' Why did she feel suddenly so frightened? she asked herself.

Randal jerked her forward into his arms and for the first time a bitter, punitive violence entered into his kiss. He bent her wild bright head back, burning her mouth with the savagery he felt, his arms an unbreakable barrier around her, his lips hard and seeking. Marcy struggled, impotent, frightened. Randal would not release her, kissing her with crushing hungriness, bruising her soft mouth. Marcy whimpered under the fierceness of his mouth, pleading with him. He drew a shaken breath, pulling back, and she turned to run, but tripped over her croquet mallet and fell headlong lying face down in the grass.

Randal sank down beside her on his knees, lifting her, turning her over gently. The smell of warm, crushed grass filled her nostrils. Randal grimaced, looking at her terrified face.

'I'm sorry,' he said roughly. 'I'm not going to hurt you, Marcy.'

She looked at him warily, her lashes fluttering, the gilt tips lying softly along her flushed cheek.

Randal made a sound in the back of his throat and began to kiss them, his lips gliding softly over her warm skin. Marcy relaxed. The touch of his mouth, the restless pressure of his hands on her back, were sensually arousing. Without understanding how she felt, she lifted her mouth, and with a groan Randal took it, parting her lips softly. Something strange seemed to be happening to her. She kept her eyes shut tight, her slender body arching towards him, quivering in the hard, desiring hands. Her hands slid round his neck. She kissed him back eagerly, and felt her own breathing begin to quicken. She could not halt the trembling in her limbs. She was hot and shuddering as Randal moved away, and with closed eyes, she moved instinctively after him, her mouth lifted in unsated need of his kiss.

Randal stared so long at her face that she opened her eyes and shyly met his look. Thickly, he said, 'Marcy, have you missed me?'

Very pink, she nodded dumbly.

His hands framed her face, his thumbs pushing into her burning bright hair. 'Marcy, I love you,' he whispered.

'Randal . . .' Her voice was its own answer, her eyes closing in surrender.

Randal lifted her against his chest, holding her, the small face pressed against his shoulder. Into her hair he whispered, 'Darling, oh, my darling, don't make me wait for years for you . . .'

She had ceased to consider consequences. She lay against him, utterly melting and pliable, pressing her cheek against his body.

He ran tender, possessive hands over her slender body, his skin warm upon her through the clinging peacock blue of the silk. 'Answer me, Marcy,' he asked into her ear, his lips playing with her small white lobe.

He caught a whisper but so muffled and incoherent

that he could make nothing of it, and pulled her away to look down into her flushed face.

'What did you say, darling?'

She slowly opened her eyes. 'You don't play fair, Randal,' she said. 'How can I make up my mind when I feel like this?'

His eyes were eager. 'Like what, Marcy?'

She looked uneasy under his searching gaze. 'I don't know. You make me feel . . . as if I was standing on the beach and a great wave came and knocked me off my feet. I can't think when I'm off balance like this.'

He grimaced. 'Marcy . . .' His sigh was grim. 'Very well, I'll go on waiting, but you're trying my patience, darling.'

She looked at him through her lashes. 'We agreed I should go to drama school.'

He gave her a disturbing smile. 'That was before,' he murmured.

'Before what?' she asked innocently.

Randal's smile was triumphant. 'Before I was sure you were beginning to want me,' he said in satisfaction.

'Oh,' she said, annoyed. 'Is that what you think, Randal?' And her flushed cheeks grew more scarlet.

He touched them with the back of his hand lovingly. 'You aren't going to pretend you don't know?' he teased.

Her eyes were frank. 'I don't know anything, Randal.'

'Then I shall have to teach you,' he said, with

immense pleasure. He lifted her to her feet, brushing grass stains off her silken skirt. 'You look as if you've been wrestling on the lawn,' he said, grinning. 'Chumble will scold like mad.'

'Oh, Randal, I like Chumble,' she said.

He grinned at her. 'She likes you. In fact, I came back early because she sent me a telegram.'

Marcy looked at him in bewilderment. 'A telegram? Why?'

His face darkened. 'Chumble was suspicious of Perry's arrival while you were here. She thought I ought to know.' He bent a cool blue gaze on her face. 'She's just been telling me that you and Perry get on like a house on fire.'

Marcy looked at him warily. 'We do,' she admitted nervously. 'I like Perry.'

Randal watched her penetratingly. 'He's not much older than you are, is he?'

'I think he's much younger,' said Marcy, with a faint giggle.

Randal's eyes relaxed in their watchful stare. 'He is a bit of an idiot.'

Marcy laughed. 'That's an understatement! He's a schoolboy at heart. Oh, but he's fun, Randal. We've had such fun, riding, playing cards, quarrelling . . . I never had a brother, and Perry is a surprise to me.'

'So long as he stays in the fraternal class,' Randal murmured. 'Brothers don't generally kiss their sisters.'

Marcy blushed.

He lifted her chin with a commanding finger. 'Did you like it when Perry kissed you?'

She met his eyes defiantly. 'Do you want me to say I didn't? Well, I did.'

Randal's face stiffened. 'Did you, Marcy?' His tone held ice.

'I like being kissed in a friendly way,' she said frankly. 'Perry is nice and he kisses nicely. I think you're being silly, Randal. I never made a fuss when you kissed me, did I? That first time?'

He stared at her, his brows drawing together. 'That's different.'

'Why?' she asked pointedly.

'I'm in love with you, Marcy,' he said soberly.

'But I wasn't in love with you,' she said, her face defiant.

That strange eagerness came into his face. 'And now, Marcy?' he asked quickly.

She bit her lip. 'You're rushing me again, Randal. Please, don't . . . give me room to breathe.'

'I must be mad,' he said harshly. 'A child just out of school who's barely been kissed in her life, and I have to fall head over heels for her!'

Marcy leaned her head against his shoulder, sensing his need for comfort. 'Poor Randal,' she murmured.

'Oh, God,' he muttered, his hands stroking her bright head. 'Oh, Marcy, you make my heart stop every time I look at you.'

She lifted her face and kissed him lightly, evading the hunger of his mouth for more. 'Come in and talk to Chumble and Lady Anne,' she told him gently. 'And smile at poor Perry. He hates the legal department so much, poor soul. Couldn't you find him a nicer place somewhere?'

'Yes,' said Randal grimly. 'Outer Mongolia or Siberia, perhaps.'

She laughed. 'Don't be a brute. Perry's petrified of you. Be nice to him.'

'If he so much as looks at you I'll cut his heart out and feed it to the pigeons in Trafalgar Square,' Randal promised. Then a frown came into his face. 'What's he doing here, anyway? Perry never had an idea in his life. What brought him down here?'

'Julia Hume,' she said softly. 'He let it out on the first day. Poor Perry was never cut out to be a conspirator.'

Randal's face grew savage. 'Did she, by God? The little . . .' The word he used made Marcy jump in shock.

'Randal!' she exclaimed, shocked. 'What awful language! Even in Paradise Street I never heard people swear quite like that!'

He grimaced. 'I'll teach that lady to keep her nose out of my life,' he said under his breath. 'If she'd succeeded in her clever little plot I'd have cut her up and fed her to the animals in the zoo . . .'

Marcy eyed him teasingly. 'What a savage pirate you are at heart, Randal,' she said softly. 'Perry said you were, and he was right. You would be at home making people walk the plank and being the terror of the seven seas.'

'And abducting all the beautiful urchins I found en route,' he said mockingly. His hand ran through her hair. 'I think it was your hair that captured my eyes— that incredible colour in the sunlight. I've seen dozens of far more beautiful women in very expensive, haute couture clothes, then I had to be knocked for six by a grubby ragamuffin in jeans!'

'I'm beginning to think you regret my jeans,' she said lightly.

'They suited your personality,' he admitted. His eyes ran over the blue silk dress. 'But in things like this you do something pretty drastic to my blood pressure, Marcy.'

She moved away, her smile backwards to him slightly provocative, 'Come and talk to Chumble, Randal . . . you've got such a one-track mind!'

CHAPTER SEVEN

PERRY was waiting apprehensively in the drawing-room with Lady Anne when they entered it with Chumble ten minutes later. Randal gave him a cool, unfriendly glance. 'How much longer are you staying, Perry?' he enquired.

Shifting nervously, Perry said with a stammer, 'W—well, I suppose I should be leaving soon.'

Chumble gave Randal a sharp look. 'He's no bother,' she informed him tartly. 'Amused Miss Marcy, he did.'

Randal looked down at Marcy. 'Did he.' The remark was more threat than question.

Marcy made a face at him. 'Stop huffing, Randal,' she said sweetly.

Perry looked at her, impressed. 'When's the marriage, Randal?' he asked, obsequiously.

'Ask the bride,' Randal snapped.

Lady Anne looked at Chumble, who gave a reproving click of her tongue. 'If you're staying here, too, Randal, I'll have to make up the blue bedroom for you.'

'I'll do it,' Marcy offered, turning to leave the room.

Randal slipped out after her, and Lady Anne looked at Chumble with a faintly harassed air. 'I wish I knew exactly what was going on between those two.'

'Marcy has Randal tied up in knots,' said Perry gleefully. 'God, you should have seen his face when he came out and saw me kiss her on the croquet lawn. I thought he was going to kill me!'

Chumble's blue lips tightened. 'You're a very silly boy, Mr Perry. One day Mr Randal will lose his temper with you. You'd better go and pack.'

'I thought you said I could stay,' he protested sulkily.

'Mr Randal was rude to you,' Chumble snapped. 'He has no business inviting guests at this house to leave. But if you're dangling after Miss Marcy you'll have to go. Anyway, Miss Anthea will be coming tomorrow, apparently, and the house will be far too full with her here.'

Perry's eyes brightened. 'Anthea coming?' He looked coaxingly at Chumble. 'Oh, let me stay, Chumble. I'll be good. I'll help to peel the potatoes for dinner, I promise.'

'Let him stay,' Lady Anne asked Chumble. 'He can amuse Anthea. Randal won't want two girls on his hands.'

Chumble snorted. 'Anthea's useless in the kitchen. All this finishing school nonsense and she can't boil an egg. Thank God for Miss Marcy!' She shuffled out mumbling to herself and Perry sat down with a sigh.

'Thanks, Aunt Anne.'

'Go and help Chumble with the potatoes,' said Lady Anne, returning to the book she was reading.

In the blue bedroom Randal lounged by the window, watching as Marcy deftly made the bed. When she had finished he caught her hand and drew her down on to it, his face urgent. 'Marcy . . .'

She wriggled in his arms like a slim eel. 'Stop it, Randal!'

'I haven't kissed you for half an hour,' he said. 'I wish to God you felt the way I did.'

She was still, looking at him seriously. 'How do you feel, Randal?'

He sighed, touching her soft skin lingeringly. 'I can't keep my hands off you. I want to be with you every waking second.' He looked at her through his dark lashes oddly. 'And all through the night, Marcy. I want to wake up and hear you breathing in the bed next to me. I want to touch you whenever I feel like it, and see you smile at me when I come into rooms . . .'

Her face was absorbed as she considered his words. They sent a quiver of response through her whole body. She could remember seeing her father come into a room and look, at once, towards her mother, and seeing her mother smile back, their exchanged looks wordlessly intimate. As a child she had often felt shut out between them. They had needed no one but each other, and she had felt excluded.

She looked up at him soberly. 'What if we had children?' she asked seriously.

Randal's eyes glowed. 'Darling,' he said urgently, reaching for her.

'Randal, listen,' she interrupted still seriously. 'How would you feel if we had a baby? Would you feel it was an intruder between us?'

'Your baby?' He smiled. 'How can you ask such a question? Any child of ours would be desperately wanted.'

A sigh came from her and she leaned her head against his shoulder.

'Anthea is arriving tomorrow,' he said, into her hair. 'You'll like her, darling.'

'I've heard a lot about her from Chumble and Perry,' she said, then she laughed. 'Perry likes her a lot.'

His face tightened. 'Good,' he said tersely.

She looked round at him. 'Don't keep scowling like that whenever I say Perry's name, Randal.'

'Stop saying it, then,' he retorted.

'Randal, if a man of your age wanted to marry Anthea, what would you think?' she asked.

He grimaced. 'I'd think he was a fool,' he said.

She gave him a curiously sober look. 'Why?'

He caught her expression and went white. 'Marcy, don't compare yourself with Anthea. She's nothing like you.' He held her so tightly she couldn't breathe, his face against her hair. 'In age you're quite close, but you have a quality she lacks. She's still a school-girl in many ways, a child.'

'So am I,' she said sadly.

Jerkily he began to speak, but Chumble came in and said crossly, 'How many times have I told you not to sit on your bed, Mr Randal? Look what you've done to it! I'm ashamed of you, Miss Marcy, letting him do it!'

They hurriedly got up and left the room with her following them, scolding them.

Randal was restless that evening, unable to take his eyes off Marcy, constantly rising and stalking about the room, refusing to play one of the noisy, quarrelsome card games she and Perry immediately launched into, his eyes brooding on her bright head.

'Do sit down, Randal,' Lady Anne sighed. 'You make me feel as if I had a tiger in the room!'

'If Randal is here, Perry won't be able to ride,' Marcy observed, slapping Perry's hand as he cheated. 'You can't play that card, you know perfectly well.'

'Do you want to ride, Randal?' Perry asked innocently. 'I expect you'll be too tired after your journey, anyway.'

'Of course I shall ride,' Randal said curtly. 'You can stay and help Chumble in the kitchen, Perry.'

Perry gave him a sulky look. 'What time is Anthea arriving?'

'Around eleven,' said Randal. 'You can drive to the station and pick her up.'

Perry cheered up. 'Okay,' he said brightly.

'If you want her to get here in one piece I wouldn't advise it,' Marcy said. 'Perry is a demon driver. He'll kill himself one day.'

'Good thing, too,' said Randal nastily.

Marcy looked round as Chumble came into the room. 'I'm just going to bed, Chumble,' she said submissively, knowing the words which were on Chumble's reproving tongue.

'And you, too, Randal,' Chumble scolded. 'You look tired. All that flying around the world isn't natural.'

Outside her room, Randal caught her hand and looked at her pleadingly. 'Darling,' he whispered, searching for her mouth.

'Goodnight, Randal,' she said firmly, slipping out

of his grip. He would not let her close her door, his eyes blazing.

'Marcy, for God's sake,' he said thickly.

She was half frightened of the look in his blue eyes. 'Please, don't, Randal,' she begged. 'Chumble will come up in a minute and get cross.'

'Oh, damn Chumble,' he snapped, pushing her against the wall, and his mouth found hers hungrily. Marcy resisted for a few seconds, then she felt that curious shivering excitement rising inside herself again, and a soft groan came from her as she relaxed against him, yielding to his body. His hands were moving over her restlessly. She felt breathless and flushed. His touch was sensitising her skin to the point where every time he touched her she felt an intense reaction of pleasure and desire.

Randal jerked the door shut with his elbow and his kiss deepened. Her arms moved round his back and pulled him closer.

'I love you,' he said hoarsely. 'Say you love me, Marcy.'

She looked at him drowsily, half dazed by her own emotions. 'I don't know,' she said, whimpering slightly, a childlike confusion in her eyes. 'Is it love? Randal, I've never known anything like this before . . . how can I be sure?'

He made an angry, hungry movement just as the door opened and Chumble came into the room, her gnarled old hands gripped crossly at her waist.

She gave Randal a furious glare. 'Well, I'm surprised at you, Randal, I really am! You know this is wrong . . . leave the child alone and get off to bed.

I'll have to speak to you tomorrow, I can see that.'

Randal ran a shaking hand through his dark hair, muttered something and vanished.

Just as flushed and taken off balance, Marcy looked at Chumble, her lips trembling, and burst suddenly into tears. Chumble looked aghast. 'Why, Miss Marcy!' She put her thin arms around the girl and patted her back, leading her to the bed. Marcy sank down, sobbing weakly. Chumble sat beside her and stroked her hair.

'Now, you tell Chumble what's going on, miss. It's time someone sorted out Mr Randal. He can be very high-handed when he gets into the mood.'

Marcy began to pour out her story through muffled sobs, and Chumble listened soberly. When Marcy had finished, Chumble lifted her head and stared closely into her wet, flushed face, reading the sweet innocent green eyes.

'So you don't know if you love him or not, then?' she asked.

Marcy gave a deep, quivering sigh. 'No,' she said. 'I . . . I've nothing to compare it with. He's so different from anyone I've ever met. Oh, Chumble, how does one know if one's in love? If I'd had a boy-friend before, or even been kissed before, I might know, but there was never anyone before Randal.'

Chumble's mouth was gentle and amused. 'When I was a girl many young girls were in your position, married to a man before they'd had time to meet anyone else, and their marriages were often very happy indeed. After all, marriage is like life . . . you have to work at it, make compromises, learn things about each other. If people tell you marriage is just love ever after, they're fooling themselves. Randal isn't going to be an easy husband, I dare say. He's not an easy man. He's had life all his own way for years. But if he's in love with you, you'll be able to manage him all right.'

A faint smile came into Marcy's green eyes. 'I know I could manage him,' she said, her mouth curving impishly. 'But do I love him?'

Chumble laughed. 'Well, now, ask yourself this . . . how would you feel if he married someone else, say, Julia Hume?'

Marcy looked stunned, then a dark red came up into her face. 'Oh,' she said breathlessly.

Chumble patted her hands. 'There, then, get yourself off to bed, Miss Marcy, and stop fussing about nothing.'

Lying in bed later Marcy thought about Julia Hume with a hardness in her small face. Julia had sent Perry down here to make trouble between herself and Randal. From what Perry had told her about Julia she was a hard, clever, very ambitious woman, and Marcy believed Randal when he told her that Julia did not love him. What was love, she asked herself thoughtfully, if it was not a true caring for the other person, a desire to help and protect them, a tenderness for them? Would she, in Julia's position, have done what Julia did? No, she thought, she would not.

Sim had kissed her and she had been flattered but

unmoved. Perry had kissed her and she had been half amused. But when Randal kissed her, she felt as if her stomach were full of butterflies.

In the morning she and Randal rode alone, Lady Anne having stayed behind in the stable to lecture Grimshaw, who was in one of his nasty recalcitrant moods, reluctant to see any of his precious horses go out of the stable that day. 'These are my horses,' Lady Anne said tartly. 'I don't keep them as ornaments. They're supposed to work.'

Randal grinned sideways at Marcy. 'Grimshaw is getting worse. He was always possessive about the horses. Now he really seems to feel they belong to him.'

'Poor Grimshaw,' said Marcy vaguely, aware of Randal's slim dark body in old riding breeches and thin silk shirt. He looked excitingly casual in those clothes. The elegant formality of his London clothes had removed him from her milieu. Now he looked quite different, and her pulses began to beat as she eyed him.

'Perry seems to have taught you to ride quite well,' Randal said, observing her with approval. 'I'll buy you a pretty little palomino,' he went on thoughtfully. 'The colouring will go well with your hair.'

'Perry rides very well,' she said softly. 'He's a fantastic jumper. He clears that hedge over there.'

Randal's jaw tightened. He gave her a furious look. 'Does he?' he asked jealously. He turned suddenly, setting his gelding at a tall holly hedge at least four feet higher than the hedge she had pointed at, and with a gasp of anxious alarm she saw him gallop towards it.

'No, Randal!' she screamed, her heart in her mouth. Randal rode on, ignoring her, and her slight body grew rigid with fear as he approached the hedge. The tall bay suddenly took off and Marcy stared, her eyes so wide they hurt, as Randal and the horse soared upward.

When she saw them clear the hedge and land the other side, a tide of icy coldness seemed to be washing over her body. She sat, staring at the great dark green hedge, shaking. Randal leapt back over the gate in the hedge and galloped towards her, a look of hard triumph in his face.

He halted, facing her, searching her white face. Marcy stared at him, so angry she could not speak for a moment. Then she slapped his face hard, her hand stinging with the blow.

Randal looked astounded.

'You might have killed yourself,' she said in quivering tones. 'What a stupid, childish, jealous trick!'

Then she turned and set Ladybird at a canter towards the house. Passing Lady Anne, she averted her face, aware that tears were running down her face, and Lady Anne looked amazed and anxious. Randal was galloping after her, his hard cheek dark red from the blow she had given him.

She took Ladybird into the stable, slid off and ran into the house, while Grimshaw muttered sullenly as he led the white horse away. Chumble looked up from the stove as she ran past, taking in her pallor and her tears. Randal rushed into the kitchen after her, but Chumble called his name in the tart nursery command which still halted him.

'Mr Randal! Where do you think you're going?'

Randal turned, fuming, his lean body tense. 'Chumble, she's upset. I . . .'

'I can see she's upset. Leave her alone,' said Chumble grimly.

Randal muttered, almost childishly, his feet scraping the floor, 'You don't understand.'

'I understand perfectly,' retorted Chumble, her tone final. 'You're harrying that child. Leave her alone for a while. You're behaving just the way you did when you were little and wanted something badly. I've told you a hundred times not to snatch. Wait until you're asked, didn't I tell you?'

He laughed reluctantly. 'This isn't nursery tea time, Chumble. It's the man who does the asking when you're grown up.'

'You've asked,' said Chumble. 'Give her time to make up her mind. Stop bullying her. She's a nice little thing and she's very confused.'

He raked a hand through his windswept hair. 'Oh, God,' he muttered, and turned and went out.

Chumble took Marcy her breakfast upstairs. Marcy had washed her tearstained face and changed. She was sitting on the floor in her room, staring at her hands, which were shaking.

'Oh,' she said, taken aback when she saw the tray. 'Chumble, there's no need . . . I was coming down. I'm sorry you had the trouble of doing this.'

'No trouble,' said Chumble. 'Now, eat a good breakfast, there's a good little girl. Anthea will be here before lunch and you'll want to make a good impression on her.'

'In her clothes?' asked Marcy wryly.

'Anthea won't mind that,' said Chumble, her face softening. 'She's a kind girl. Silly at times, but good-hearted.'

Marcy looked at her through her lashes. 'Did Randal come in?'

Chumble looked sour. 'I sent him off with a flea in his ear.'

'He behaved very badly,' said Marcy. 'He deliberately took a dangerous jump just to show off because I said Perry rode well.'

Chumble gave her a curious look. 'What did you say to him?'

'I hit him as hard as I could,' Marcy admitted, her face defiant.

'Ah,' said Chumble, smiling. 'Then you burst into tears and ran away, did you?'

Marcy blushed. 'Oh, Chumble, I think I must be in love. I felt so frightened when he took that jump. I thought I would die if anything happened to him, and I was so mad when he rode up, grinning like a fool, that I could have killed him!'

Chumble smiled lovingly at her. 'Eat your breakfast, Miss Marcy. I'll keep him busy downstairs, don't worry.'

Marcy ate as much as she could, but her appetite had oddly deserted her, and she sat brooding in her room until she heard the sound of voices in the hall, and guessed Anthea had arrived. Slowly, nervously, she went out and began to go downstairs.

Randal was in the hall, kissing a dark girl of her own age, but at the sound of her arrival he turned, his face flushed and anxious, to look at her, and the girl beside him stared, too.

Ignoring Randal, Marcy smiled at her as she joined them. Anthea was slim and elegant in a pale. blue linen suit, her dark hair softly curling around a fresh-coloured face. Blue eyes like Randal's looked Marcy up and down, and a puzzled look came into her face as she took stock of the cream dress Marcy was wearing.

'Yes,' said Marcy frankly, 'It's yours. Randal didn't like my clothes, so he insisted I borrowed some of yours. I'm sorry.'

Anthea gave a faint giggle. 'I don't mind,' she said. 'It looks very good on you. Keep them. I've spent a fortune on new ones in Geneva and I shall have to throw out some of the clothes I had before to make room for them.' She gave Randal a saucy look. 'I overdrew my allowance, brother dear, but as you're radiantly happy you won't mind, will you?'

Randal wasn't even looking at her. His blue eyes on Marcy's averted face, he was intent on studying her.

Anthea gave another little giggle. 'I was dreading telling him how much I owe all the way from Switzerland,' she told Marcy. 'What a relief now it's over! I've been reading all about you in the English papers, and Perry tells me you're fun. You're in my room, aren't you? Is Chumble putting me in the airing cupboard?'

'No,' said Marcy. 'Come on and I'll show you where you're sleeping. Then I must go and help

Chumble get lunch. She's overworked with so many of us in the house.'

Anthea groaned. 'I hope that doesn't mean I have to help with cooking. Perry tells me he's been peeling potatoes. This I must see!'

'Even worse, you'll have to eat them,' said Marcy. 'He leaves lots of peel and eyes on them.'

The two girls went upstairs talking together while Perry, puffing bitterly, staggered in with Anthea's luggage. He shouted after her, 'Why didn't you bring a whole planeload while you were at it? What have you got in them? Rocks?'

'I told you to take body-building exercises,' Marcy informed him over her shoulder, saying confidentially to Anthea, 'Poor Perry, he's so out of condition. All he does is drive around in that crazy car of his and spend all his income on piranhas.'

'Piranhas?' asked Anthea incredulously.

'Girls,' Marcy explained. 'They like high life, apparently, and once he's spent his all on them they vanish.'

Anthea looked back at Perry. 'Silly idiot!'

'Isn't he?' Marcy grinned. She threw open the door of the room designed for Anthea. 'I made up the bed for you.'

Anthea bounced on the mattress. 'Oh, lovely, feathers! I'll just sink into them as if I was in a snow-drift.'

'Did you ski in Switzerland much?' Marcy asked.

'Every day,' Anthea nodded. 'Do you ski?'

'I don't do anything except help Chumble with the

lunch,' Marcy laughed. 'And I must do that now, I'm afraid. I'll see you later.'

Anthea's voice halted her as she reached the door. 'Are you really going to marry Randal?'

Marcy looked back at her, her green eyes sober. 'Would you mind if I did?'

'Good lord, no. You seem to fit in beautifully,' said Anthea. 'Perry's a fathead, but I trust his judgment on some things, and he sings your praises very highly.'

Marcy smiled. 'I like him, too.' And she vanished without another word

Perry was sulkily peeling potatoes in the kitchen when she arrived. She gave him a grin and began to help Chumble. Randal wandered into the room and was chased out at once by Chumble's irate voice.

'Too many people in this room already, Randal. Go and chase your sister up. Lunch will be ready in ten minutes.'

It was a cheerful, noisy meal. Perry and Anthea began a long argument about a pop star during the second course, and their loud voices drowned Randal's intent silence, and Marcy's quiet conversation with Lady Anne about Grimshaw.

Afterwards, Perry volunteered Anthea to help with the washing up, and was counter-volunteered by her, in revenge, to help with the drying up. Chumble swept them both away with her, softly chiding them, as they squabbled.

Lady Anne put a hand to her head. 'I think I'll walk down to the village—I need some fresh air. Randal, much as I love your sister, if she and Perry are going to make that racket all the time I shall be very relieved when she leaves.'

Left alone, Marcy got up to escape, but Randal caught her hand. 'I'm sorry I made such a fool of myself over that jump,' he said huskily. 'It was a stupid thing to do, but I've taken it before, darling. I hunt, you know. I wasn't being completely crazy.'

She wriggled her hand out of his grip and went out into the garden, breathing in the soft summer afternoon, the fragrance of the roses giving that warm scented sweetness to the whole garden.

Wandering down through the lawns to the round goldfish pond, she sat down on the low whitestone wall, staring at the dark green lily pads with their smooth white flowers.

On the surface of the water Randal's face was outlined shadowily as he joined her. He sat down, staring at her profile.

'Are you very angry with me?' he asked humbly.

'I was,' she said, sliding one thin finger into the water and flicking the cool drops over the pond.

He bent and kissed her elbow softly. 'Forgive me,' he whispered, kissing it again.

Marcy turned, flicking water at him teasingly. 'Make me,' she said breathlessly.

Randal's face changed, and an incredulous passion came into his blue eyes. He pulled her towards him, and Marcy surrendered, knowing exactly what she was doing, her whole slender body given to him, her lashes fluttering against her cheeks, her heart thudding.

His kiss sent quivers of wild excitement along he

veins. She kissed him back, winding her slender arms around his neck. Against her mouth he murmured her name.

'I love you,' he whispered.

She drew back her mouth, looking up at him through her lashes, seeing the restless, eager look on his tough face.

'I love you, Randal,' she said softly.

For a moment he was still, breathing more and more heavily, then his mouth swept down to her and his arms held her so hard she couldn't breathe.

Later, he looked down at the lily pond, and a grin came into his face. 'How apt it should be here,' he said to himself.

She was puzzled. 'Why?'

He stroked her cheek with a finger. 'I'll show you one day,' he said. 'When will you marry me, Marcy?'

'When you like,' she said, knowing it no longer mattered to her that she had known so little of life before she met him. When he risked his life to jump the holly hedge she had known in a flash that anything else she found in life would have no validity apart from him.

He laughed huskily. 'My God, you're tempting me! I'd say tomorrow, but I doubt if the family would approve. I suppose it will have to be the full works.'

She looked alarmed. 'Oh, no, Randal. Can't we just get married?'

'That's how I would like it,' he agreed. 'But what about everyone else? Anthea is no doubt already planning her wedding outfit.'

'I'd like to get married in the church in the village,'

she said. 'A quiet wedding with just a few people there.'

Randal gazed at her, his heart in his eyes. 'Sure you wouldn't regret a big London wedding?'

'I'd hate it,' she admitted.

His face set obstinately. 'Then a quiet country wedding it shall be, my love. When?'

She leaned her head against his shoulder. 'As soon as possible,' she said.

His arms held her, his hand possessive on her bright hair. 'Yes,' he said huskily, 'as soon as possible.'

It did not work out exactly as planned. Marcy's own warm nature made it impossible from the start. When a list of guests was discussed she insisted on inviting Sim and Lisa, Russell, Wesley and his mother, Dost Mohammed and a dozen others. Randal wanted to argue, but he was too intent on getting the wedding over. A busload of Paradise Street was to arrive. Anthea and Perry helped with the family list, which began to grow at an alarming rate, as distant cousins in outer Britain were put down as essential guests. Randal looked more and more grim.

'Quiet wedding?' he murmured. 'It's going to be a riot!'

He had to return to London, leaving Anthea and Marcy staying at Lady Anne's, relieved that at least Perry had gone back to work. Julia Hume winkled out of Perry enough of the picture to be icily restrained when she spoke to Randal, contenting herself with a few smiling asides referring to Marcy's age and odd friends. Randal bore these with equanimity, inwardly intent upon the last kiss he had exchanged with Marcy, remembering with sickening hunger the softness of her body in his arms and the look she had given him.

The Campion Project was well on the way to being finalised as the architect drew up plans which left the site as a central core to the whole of the new development. Andrew McAllister, summoned to see Randal, was crisply warned against the sort of behind-the-scenes dealing he had been involved in, and left chastened and sullen. The press, through Russell, pursued Marcy to Somerset, but drew a blank when Grimshaw, growling like a wild bear, chased them off the ground with a pitchfork, threatening to bring out a shotgun if they came back.

Anthea and Marcy rapidly made friends as the wedding plans progressed. Anthea helped Marcy to choose the design of her wedding dress, watched as she underwent fittings, exclaimed with delight as she saw her in the finished dress and was thrilled about her own bridesmaid's dress. Marcy had decided to have just one bridesmaid. She had no girl friends of her own to choose from among.

'You could have Perry as a pageboy,' Anthea giggled.

The two girls fell about, laughing, and Chumble gave them a glance of indulgent despair.

It was a warm summer morning when Marcy stood in the bedroom at the Somerset house, as slender as a flower, in her white dress of lace and silk, watching as Chumble tenderly pressed the crown of lily of the valley and pearls down over her long veil, her gnarled fingers shaking.

'You're white, child,' she said, gazing into Marcy's small face.

'I'm petrified,' Marcy gasped, trying to smile.

Chumble produced a small silver flask. 'You take a small glass of this, Miss Marcy. I remember Miss Natalie shaking like a leaf on her wedding day and it steadied her.'

Marcy giggled. 'You don't want me to be drunk on my wedding day, Chumble.'

Chumble pressed the small glass to her lips. The fiery liquid made her choke, then it ran through her veins. 'Brandy,' she said, laughing.

Marcy was to be given away by Sim. He was waiting in the hall, very distinguished in frock coat and silver-grey hat, as she came down the stairs.

Her selection of him to give her away had brought out one of Randal's brief moments of jealousy, but she had soothed it away easily enough, and now she smiled at Sim, the wide, radiant, childlike smile which made her small face so beautiful.

Sim had tears in his eyes as he pressed her hand against his arm in the wedding car. 'Lisa's pregnant,' he whispered. 'She's expecting in the spring.'

Marcy turned her smile to him, her eyes glowing with pleasure. 'Oh, I'm so glad, Sim!'

'Mark if it's a boy, Marcy if it's a girl,' he said, as he had told her before.

'And is your mother happy?'

'Happy?' His eyes danced. 'Her fingers ache from knitting baby shoes and coats! She nags Lisa ragged about iron pills and afternoon rests. And Russell's beginning to have a hunted look because every time she sees him she begins to talk about Michelle.'

Marcy laughed. 'I miss Paradise Street. I was happy there,' she said with a sigh.

Sim gave her an odd glance. 'Aren't you happy now, Marcy?' His eyes were worried.

Her face shone. 'Happy? Oh, Sim, I'm so happy I'm afraid. It seems so incredible, the way I feel, that I can't help thinking it's a dream.'

He smiled tenderly. 'He's kept all his promises, your man. The Campion Project is going to make a big difference to Paradise Street. Somewhere for the kids to play, for the adults to meet. He's a lot more human than I ever suspected.'

Her smile was filled with secrets. 'Yes, Randal's very human,' she agreed.

'Lucky, too,' Sim added doggedly. 'He already had everything life could offer him. Now he's got you, too.'

Marcy looked down at the floating bridal lace and silk, the delicacy of her bouquet, and her heart thudded as she thought of the night ahead. The wedding was merely a bridge—the path by which she and Randal could come to the moment of utter happiness when they would belong together. She wished it was over already.

She walked into the small village church through a throng of smiling, curious faces and a battery of cameras which flashed around her, lighting the summer morning air.

The organ began to play and she walked down the narrow aisle of the packed congregation towards Randal's dark head, her knees trembling, making each step an effort. Randal turned slightly and he looked at her, his face so white she thought he must be going to faint, but there was a blaze of triumph in the blue eyes which reminded her oddly of the moment when he rode back to her after taking the tall holly hedge.

The service began and, like a soft-voiced child, she repeated the words and performed the actions she had been taught, feeling Randal's hand shake as he slid the ring on to her thin finger.

Walking back out of the church some time later she saw faces which smiled at her, and somehow she smiled back, although she was trembling with nerves. Wesley's wide grin she remembered for a long time, his impudent grin and wink, as though he considered her clever to have pulled off such a coup.

'You ain't going to forget Paradise Street, are you, Marcy?' asked Luke Green during the noisy, crowded reception. 'You'll come and see us all some time?'

She nodded seriously. 'Campion House is my family house, don't forget, Luke. I want to make sure it's used for the people of Paradise Street from now on, especially the children. No more playing around dustbins if I can help it . . .'

Chumble sought her out a while later and whispered, 'Time to change, child.'

Obediently Marcy followed her upstairs. Anthea

wanted to come, but Chumble said firmly, 'Marcy's over-excited as it is, Anthea. Go and tease Perry, but leave her alone.'

In the quiet bedroom she stood childlike as Chumble helped her to shed the pure white lace and silk wedding dress, watching as Chumble carefully wrapped it in tissue paper and laid it on the bed. 'You looked beautiful,' Chumble said with a sigh.

'Oh, Chumble,' she said excitedly, her face flushed, 'I'm so nervous!'

Chumble slid her into the elegant little green dress and coat she was wearing to go on her honeymoon, her gnarled hands gentle. 'Randal will look after you,' she said. 'Trust Randal.'

'I do,' said Marcy, her breath catching.

She barely noticed the next few moments as they somehow fought their way to the silver-blue limousine through photographers, reporters and guests. She was shivering with fright, tense and nervous, as the car finally drove away, clattering because Perry had fastened a collection of tin cans, kettles and old boots to it with string.

'Damn him,' said Randal under his breath, but drove on, with the clatter following them. 'We'll have to search the luggage carefully. I've no doubt he's filled the cases with confetti.'

'I expect Anthea did that,' said Marcy, giggling. 'They work as a team.'

'My sister's nearly as crazy as he is,' said Randal.

'If you don't watch out, Perry will marry her,' Marcy murmured.

Randal swore and she jumped. 'Randal!'

'You're kidding, of course,' he said, 'The idea turns one's brain to jelly.'

Marcy wasn't kidding. But she said nothing. She somehow didn't imagine Perry was in any hurry to settle down, and certainly Anthea was eager to launch herself on the joys of London before she even considered the future. Her suspicions might be wildly inaccurate. If they weren't . . . well, time would solve that problem. No point in upsetting Randal at this juncture.

He drove into a layby and cut the strings Perry had tied to the bumper, throwing the objects into a handy trash can, then he climbed back into the car and glanced at her.

'Where are we going for our honeymoon?' she asked him shyly. 'You still haven't told me.'

He grinned at her. 'A farmhouse which belongs to a friend of mine,' he said. 'Half an hour from here. It's remote and peaceful and not a soul will find us.' Then he started the car again and drove on, whistling between his teeth.

She eyed him with Chumble's grim air of reproof. 'I distinctly heard you tell Russell we were going abroad!'

'Teach him to ask questions,' said Randal, unabashed.

'You're quite ruthless, aren't you?' she murmured, a faint smile on her face.

'Totally,' he agreed cheerfully.

'What if I said I would have preferred to go abroad?'

He looked at her in dismay. 'Would you?'

Her green eyes teased him. 'No,' she admitted demurely.

He gave her a narrow-eyed look. 'Torment,' he said huskily, and for a while they were silent.

The farmhouse was set in a wide acreage of grazing land on which the mild white shapes of sheep could be seen slowly moving through intermediate hedges. They drove up a narrow hedged lane and parked in the cobbled yard at the side of the house. While Marcy was putting on the kettle, Randal moved their cases into the house and garaged the car out of sight. They drank a cup of tea then went up to inspect the rest of the house. It was a cosy, old-fashioned farm-house with spacious rooms and a large grandfather clock ticking somnolently in the wide hall.

'I love it,' said Marcy, staring out of the bedroom window.

Randal lay down on the bed, his arms under his head, watching her. She turned and caught the look on his face and her breath caught.

'Come here,' he said huskily.

'I've got to get the supper,' she protested. 'You'll be hungry.'

'I couldn't eat a damned thing,' he said, holding out his hand. 'Come here, Marcy. I'm not waiting for another second. I want you now.'

She sat down on the bed beside him, her hand in his, watching as he carried it to his lips and kissed the blue vein inside her wrist.

'I love you more than I've ever loved anyone or anything in the world,' he said softly.

She looked through her gold-tipped lashes at him.

'I love you the same way,' she said, faintly surprised. 'I didn't want to—I didn't want life to hand me a present so soon. I was looking forward to finding out at leisure about life and people . . . then wham! You just put me in your pocket and here I am . . .'

'Sorry, Marcy?' he asked wryly, a look of faint anxiety on his hard face.

She leaned slowly towards him, her eyes holding his, and let her mouth brush against his, feeling his lips tremble under her touch. 'No,' she whispered. 'Oh, no, Randal darling . . .'

He held his breath for a second, then pulled her down on to the bed, his hands hungrily possessive. She surrendered softly to his eager mouth, and they lay, kissing, their hands touching each other with increasingly restless passion.

Randal buried his face in the side of her slender neck. She could hear his heart beating jerkily against her. 'I'm almost afraid to touch you,' he whispered thickly. 'Marcy, you're so young, and I couldn't bear to hurt or frighten you.'

'Frightened of the last fence, Randal?' she asked gently. She sat up while he rolled over on to his back, staring at her anxiously. Slowly she lifted her arms and unzipped her dress, and Randal's breath caught audibly. A little flushed, shaking slightly, Marcy shed the rest of her clothes. Randal had not moved. His blue eyes moved over her flickeringly, and she wondered why he was lying there so still. A faint worry came into her mind. Didn't he want her, after all?

Even as she thought it, he pulled her down into his

arms and answered her question with the fire of his hunger unleashed at last, his arms and mouth desperately out of control, as though the chain on which he had held himself had snapped.

A slight fear entered Marcy's mind as she submitted to his passionate caresses. She was so untutored in the ways of love. Would she disappoint him now? Could a girl of her age satisfy a man like Randal?

Moments later, softly moaning her own pleasure in his hard arms, all fear and question had been forgotten as Randal possessed her. Randal kissed her white throat, shaking, as the slender body in his arms became a flame and sent his own desire soaring beyond any heights he had ever reached before. He pushed back her wild, bright hair, his blue eyes feverish as he looked at her, and saw the glaze of answering passion in her glance.

Beyond the window the summer sky drew down to evening, and the white sheep safely grazed on the open pastures.

A year later Marcy, in T-shirt and yellow jeans, sat on the lawn of Lady Anne's house, her wild bright hair in disorder, watching as Perry crawled across the grass, growling like a bear.

'He isn't old enough to play with you yet, Perry,' Marcy said, grinning. In the small wicker crib by her side lay something which had tiny starfish hands and a bubble-blowing mouth. Perry peered over the crib and said it wasn't fair.

'What isn't?' Marcy asked, weaving a yellow buttercup into her own hair.

'Ever since you got married Julia's been hounding me to death. Marcy, angel, do get Randal to move me.'

Marcy wove another buttercup into her mop. 'I'll ask him again!' she promised. She suspected Randal had been deliberately leaving Perry in the legal department to annoy Julia.

'Anthea will be down at six,' she said. 'Go and fetch her from the station, there's a darling, Perry. And do try to drive more carefully. We want Anthea to get here in a condition to eat dinner.'

'Funny!' said Perry, moving off reluctantly.

He passed Randal on the way to the house and got a quick, wry look which made him grimace. Randal joined his wife and son and stared from one to the other with amusement.

'I don't know which of you is the older,' he said, sinking down on to the grass beside her. 'Who's been putting flowers in your hair? Not Perry, I hope?'

She gave him her provocative, teasing smile. 'Why don't you move poor Perry out of Julia's slave camp? She's driving him mad.'

'He's driving her mad,' said Randal pleasurably.

'Who cares about her? Think of poor Perry. Can't you give him a job in the New York office?'

Randal looked at her through his dark lashes. 'Why New York? Is he bothering you, Marcy?'

She knelt up and threaded a buttercup through his dark hair, her hands intimate and tormenting. 'Don't get jealous at the slightest thing! No, I'm just thinking that it might be best if he was out of the country for the next year while Anthea has her fling.'

He looked aghast. 'You're not still harping on Anthea and Perry? I'd strangle her before I let her marry Perry!'

'Darling, she and Perry are soulmates,' Marcy said gently. 'Just get Perry off to New York while Anthea has time to take a last look around before she decides on him.'

A dark frown came into Randal's face. 'Do you regret having had no fling before you married me, Marcy?' His voice was quiet and heavy.

She suddenly pushed him backwards on to the soft warm grass and lay on top of him, kissing him until his arms came up possessively to hold her tightly.

'The question is: do you regret having married a ragamuffin in yellow jeans?' she asked, tickling his nose with a buttercup.

'I'm crazy about you, and you know it,' he said, laughing.

'Right answer,' she said, her mouth impudent. 'Any other, and you'd be forced to peel the potatoes for dinner, which is what I've got to go and do now before Chumble comes out to scold me. I love staying here, though. It's so much more like home than our house. Anatole won't let me help with the dinner and Walters looks scandalised if I open the front door or answer the phone.'

'They both dote on you openly,' said Randal, grinning. 'You run that house with a smile and a word.' He glanced into the crib. 'Should James be making those funny noises?'

'Yes, he likes it,' she said, unconcerned.

'He sounds as if he's being sick,' said Randal, watching the tiny fingers wriggle.

'He's singing,' she said indignantly.

Randal looked at her, his blue eyes passionate. 'Darling Marcy, you're so young to have a child . . . I'd no right to pick you up and carry you off as I did before you'd had a chance to live.'

'Pirates do that sort of thing,' said Marcy cheerfully. 'Me, I'm all for being abducted by a pirate. It makes life so interesting.' Her gold-tipped lashes fluttered at him. 'Especially now I'm no longer walking about with a pillow up my smock.'

He grinned. 'You wanton!' He pulled her back on to the grass and they rolled over, kissing, their arms around each other.

'Mr Randal,' said Chumble disapprovingly, 'you're alarming baby!'

'Oh, God!' groaned Randal, lying on his back with a grin.

Chumble gave him a glare. 'Carry the crib into the house at once. Baby needs his bath.'

'Yes, Chumble,' said Randal, obeying.

Chumble turned her grim attention to Marcy. 'You're wearing those nasty jeans again, miss. When you've changed you can come down and help me with the dinner.'

'Yes, Chumble,' Marcy said submissively.

'And you've got buttercups in your hair,' said Chumble, shaking her head. 'Don't bring them into the house. I don't want a mess on my carpets.'

Randal laughed as Marcy obediently pulled out the offending flowers and strewed them on the lawn, then catching Chumble's eye, he walked towards the house with the crib. Marcy caught up with him and leaned her slender shoulder against him as they walked. Randal turned loving blue eyes on her.

'I love you with buttercups in your hair and yellow jeans on,' he whispered.

'Ssh! Chumble will hear you,' she replied.

'Damn Chumble,' he said. 'Damn the whole world. I love you, Marcy, buttercups, yellow jeans and all, and I don't care who knows it.'

Harlequin
Presents...

The beauty of true romance...
The excitement of world travel...
The splendor of first love...

unique love stories for today's woman

Harlequin Presents...
novels of honest,
twentieth-century love,
with characters who
are interesting, vibrant
and alive.

The elegance of love...
The warmth of romance...
The lure of faraway places...

Six new novels, every
month — wherever
paperbacks are sold.